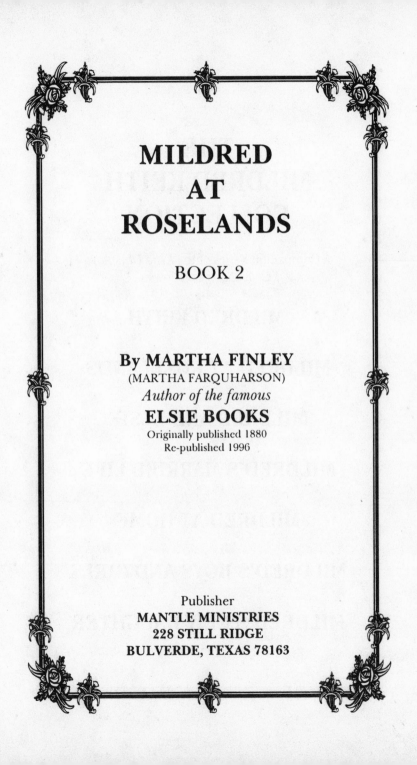

MILDRED
AT
ROSELANDS

BOOK 2

By MARTHA FINLEY
(MARTHA FARQUHARSON)
Author of the famous
ELSIE BOOKS
Originally published 1880
Re-published 1996

Publisher
MANTLE MINISTRIES
228 STILL RIDGE
BULVERDE, TEXAS 78163

THE MILDRED KEITH COLLECTION

A Companion Series of the *Elsie Dinsmore Collections* as follows:

MILDRED KEITH

MILDRED AT ROSELANDS

MILDRED AND ELSIE

MILDRED'S MARRIED LIFE

MILDRED AT HOME

MILDRED'S BOYS AND GIRLS

MILDRED'S NEW DAUGHTER

AUTHOR'S PREFACE

The Keith family were relatives of Horace Dinsmore, and as my readers will observe, the date of this story is some seven years earlier than that of the first *Elsie* book.

The journey, [detailed in **Mildred Keith: Book 1**] and that most sickly season, which I have attempted to describe, were events in my own early childhood. The latter still dwells in my memory as a dreadful dream.

Our family—a large one—were all down with the fever except my aged grandmother and a little sister of six or seven, and "help could not be had for love or money."

My father, who was a physician, kept up and made his rounds among his town and country patients for days after the fever had attacked him, but was at length compelled to take his bed, and I well remember lying there beside him while the neighbors flocked into the room to consult him about their sick ones at home.

That region of country is now, I believe, as healthy as almost any other part of our favored land. Such a season, it was said, had never been known before, and there has been none like it since.

Martha Finley

MILDRED AT ROSELANDS.

Chapter First.

"Prayer ardent opens heaven."

—YOUNG.

IT was near noon of a bright warm day early in October. Mrs. Keith was alone in her pretty sitting-room, busily plying her needle at the open window looking out upon the river.

Occasionally she lifted her head and sent a quick, admiring glance at its bright, swiftly-flowing waters and the woods beyond, beautiful and gorgeous in their rich autumnal robes.

There was a drowsy hum of insects in the air; and mingling with it the cackle of a rejoicing hen, the crowing of a cock and other rural sounds; the prattle of childish voices too came pleasantly to her ear, from the garden behind the house where the little ones were at play, calling, once and again, a tender, motherly smile to her lips.

Yet a slight cloud of care rested on her usually calm and placid features and thought seemed very busy in her brain.

It was of Mildred she was thinking. Father and mother both had noticed with a good deal of anxiety, that the young girl did not recover fully from the severe strain of the long weeks of nursing that had fallen to her lot during the past summer.

She was much paler and thinner than her wont, had frequent headaches and seemed weak and languid, a very little exertion causing excessive fatigue.

Only last night they had lain awake an hour or more talking about it, and consulting together as to what could be done for the "dear child."

They feared the severity of the coming winter would increase her malady, and wished very much that they could send her away for some months, or a year, to a milder climate; but the difficulty—apparently an insuperable one—was to find means.

It took no small amount to feed, clothe and educate such a family as theirs, and sickness had made this year one of unusual expense.

As the loving mother sat there alone she had turned over in her mind plan after plan for accomplishing this, which for her child's good, she so ardently desired to do ; but only to reject each in turn as utterly impracticable.

Aunt Wealthy, she knew, would gladly receive Mildred into her pleasant home for as long a time as her parents might be willing to spare her; but still there was the money to be provided for the journey, and besides a yet milder climate than that of Lansdale was desirable.

But the slight cloud lifted from Mrs. Keith's brow, and a sweet expression of perfect peace and content took its place as she bethought of her best Friend and His infinite love and power. He could clear away all these difficulties and would do so in answer to prayer, if in His unerring wisdom He saw that it would be for their real good—their truest happiness.

Her heart went up to him in a silent petition ; and then a sweet, glad song of praise burst half unconsciously from her lips.

As she ceased a rap at the door into the hall --which as well as the outer one, stood wide open—caught her ear.

She turned her head to see a tall gentleman, a fine looking, middle-aged man standing there and regarding her with a pleased smile.

" Uncle Dinsmore ! is it possible !   Oh how glad I am to see you ! " she cried, dropping her work and springing toward him with both hands extended.

He took them, drew her to him and kissing her affectionately, first on one cheek, then on the other, said gayly, " I flattered myself you would be, else I should not have traveled some hundreds of miles for the express purpose of paying you a visit.   Fair and sweet as ever, Marcia !   Time deals more gently with you than is his wont with the most of the world."

" Ah, I remember you as always given to pretty compliments," she returned, with a pleased, but half incredulous smile, as she drew forward the most comfortable chair in the room and made him seat himself therein, while she relieved him of his hat and cane.

" So I have taken you by surprise ? " he said inquiringly and with a satisfied look.

"I did not even know you were at the North.   When did you leave Roselands ?   Were they all well ?   Are any of them with you ?"

" One question at a time, Marcia," he said with a good-humored laugh. "I left home in June, bringing all the family with me as far as Philadelphia.   They are visiting now in eastern Pennsylvania.   I went on to New York a month ago to see Horace off for Europe, then concluded to come on into Ohio and Indiana, to have a look at this great western country, your Aunt Wealthy and yourself. I purpose spending a week or two with you, if quite convenient and agreeable, then to return, taking Lansdale in my way, and paying a short visit there."

"Convenient and agreeable!" she cried, with a joyous laugh, and glad tears shining in her eyes, "sunlight was never more welcome, and the longer you stay, the better. You came by the stage? Where is your luggage?"

"Yes, by the stage. My valise is—Ah!" half rising from his chair, with extended hand, as a handsome, intelligent looking lad of fifteen or sixteen, in working dress, but neat and clean, came in from the hall, carrying a valise.

"I found this on the porch," he began, but broke off abruptly at sight of the stranger.

"Rupert, our eldest son," said Mrs. Keith, with a glance full of motherly pride directed toward the lad. "Rupert, this is Uncle Dinsmore, your Cousin Horace's father."

The two shook hands warmly, Rupert saying, "I am very glad to see you, sir, I have heard mother speak of you so often."

The gentleman answering, "Thank you, my boy. Yes, your mother and I are very old

friends, though I am older than she, by a score
of years or more."

"That must be your uncle's, Rupert, take
it to the spare room," said Mrs. Keith, glancing at the valise."

"A fine looking fellow, but all Keith, isn't
he, Marcia?" remarked her uncle, as the lad
left the room. Then as Cyril bounded in at
another door, "Ah! this one's a Stanhope!
Come and shake hands with your uncle, my
man."

Don and the two little girls were close behind Cyril, and these had scarcely been intro-
duced, when Mr. Keith came in from his office,
bringing with him Mildred, Zillah and Ada,
whom he had met on the way.

Mr. Dinsmore was a stranger to them all,
but every one seemed glad that he had come
to visit them, and he was quite charmed with
the cordiality of his reception, and the bright,
intelligent faces, and refined manners of both
parents and children.

They made him very welcome, very com
fortable, and spared no exertion for his enter
tainment.

Being an observant man, he soon discovered
that Mildred, toward whom he felt specially
drawn from the first, was ailing, and immedi

ately proposed taking her home with him to spend the winter in the sunny South.

This was on the afternoon of the day succeeding that of his arrival, as he and Mr. and Mrs. Keith sat conversing together in the parlor, the young people having scattered to their work or play.

The father and mother exchanged glances, each reading in the other's face a longing desire to accept the invitation for their child, mingled with the sad conviction that it was impossible to do so.

This Mr. Keith presently put into words, accompanied with warm thanks for the intended kindness to Mildred.

"Tut, tut," said Mr. Dinsmore, "don't talk of kindness, the obligation will be on my part; and as to the impossibility, it is all in your imaginations. I, of course, shall bear all the expense of the journey, and—No, Marcia, don't interrupt me. I owe it to you, for I can never repay the kindness you showed your aunt in her last sickness, and to poor Horace and myself after she was gone. And you owe it to your child not to refuse for her what is really necessary to her restoration to health."

"Dear uncle, you are most kind, you must let me say it," said Mrs. Keith, with tears in her eyes. " I will not deny that the expense is the greatest obstacle, for the family purse is low at present, and I will not let my pride stand in the way of the acceptance of your generous offer, but there are other difficulties. I do not see how I could get her ready in the few days to which you have limited your visit here."

" I'll stretch it to a fortnight, then, if that'll answer," he returned, in a short, quick, determined way, that bespoke him little used to opposition to his will. " Besides," he went on, " what need of so much preparation? purchases can be made to much better advantage in Philadelphia, and sewing done at Roselands, where we have two accomplished seamstresses among the servants. I've heard Mrs. Dinsmore boast that one of them can cut and fit, make and trim a dress as well as any mantuamaker she ever saw."

Mrs. Keith expressed a lively sense of his kindness, but suggested that in all probability Mrs. Dinsmore found plenty of employment for the two women in sewing for herself and family.

Her uncle scouted the idea, asserting that they had not enough to do to keep them out of mischief.

Mrs. Keith was driven from her last refuge of excuse, and truth to tell was not sorry to have it so. Mr. Keith gave consent, Mildred was summoned and the plan laid before her to her great astonishment and delight.

" Oh, Uncle Dinsmore, how kind ! " she exclaimed, her cheeks flushing, her eyes sparkling. " It seems too good to be true, that I shall see Roselands, the beautiful place mother has so often described to us ! But no, no, it will never do for me to go and leave mother to bear the cares and burdens of housekeeping and the children all alone ! " she cried with sudden change of tone. " How could I be so selfish as to think of it for a single moment. Mother dear, I don't want to go, indeed I do not."

" But my dear child, I want you to go," Mrs. Keith said, smiling through unshed tears. " You need rest and change of scene ; and though I shall miss you sadly, I shall enjoy the thought that you are gaining in many ways, and in the prospect of soon having you at home again."

" Yes," said Mr. Dinsmore, " travel is improving, and you can go on with your studies at Roselands if you fancy doing so : we have an excellent, thoroughly educated lady as governess, and masters coming from the city twice a

week to give instruction in music and drawing
You shall share their attentions if you will.

"Come, it is not worth while to raise ob-
jections; for I can overrule them all, and am
quite determined to carry my point.

'Mr. Keith," he added, rising and looking
about for his hat, "suppose we take a walk
round the town, leaving the ladies to talk over
the necessary arrangements."

The gentlemen went out together, but the
next moment Mr. Dinsmore stepped back again
to hand Mrs. Keith a letter, saying, as he did so,

"I owe you an apology, Marcia, for my forgetfulness. Horace entrusted this to my care
and it should have been given you immediately
on my arrival. Au revoir, ladies!" and with a
courtly bow he was gone.

Mrs. Keith broke the seal and unfolded the
sheet. There was an enclosure, but she did
not look at it until she had read the note, which
she did almost at a glance, for it was plainly
written and very brief.

Dear Marcia.—Excuse a hasty line, as I am
going aboard the steamer which is to carry me
to Europe.

"I know my father wants to take Mildred
with him on his return to Roselands. I hope

you will let her go, and that you will do me the great kindness of accepting the enclosed trifle, to be used in providing her with an outfit such as you may deem suitable. It is a very small part of the debt I have owed you ever since the death of my loved mother.

Your affectionate cousin,

HORACE DINSMORE."

"The dear generous fellow!" she exclaimed, tears starting to her eyes: then as she unfolded the bank note, "A trifle, indeed! Mildred, child, it is a hundred dollars!" and the tears rolled down her cheeks.

"But you will not take it, mother, surely?" said Mildred, her cheeks flushing hotly; her pride up in arms at once at the thought of coming under such an obligation, even to a relative.

"My child," said Mrs. Keith, "I could not bear to hurt him as I well know he would be hurt by a rejection of his kindness. We will accept it: if not as a gift, as a loan to be repaid some day when we are able. Another reason why I feel that we ought not to let pride lead us to refuse this, is that it seems to have come— it and your uncle's invitation also—so directly in answer to prayer."

She went on to tell Mildred of their anxiety in regard to her, and in particular of the petitions she had been putting up on her behalf, just before Mr. Dinsmore's arrival.

"Ah!" she said in conclusion, "how good is our God! He has fulfilled to me his gracious promise, 'And it shall come to pass, that before they call, I will answer, and while they are yet speaking, I will hear.'"

A moment's silence, then Mildred said in half tremulous tones, "Oh, it is a blessed thing to trust in God! I hope my faith will grow to be as strong as yours, mother, and I hope I am thankful for this money, but—mother, am I very wicked to feel it something of a trial to have to take it?"

"I hope not," Mrs. Keith answered, with a smile and a sigh, "I do not want to see my children too ready to take help from others. I trust they will always prefer any honest work by which they may earn their bread, to a life of luxury and ease and dependence. That they will always remember the command, 'Every man shall bear his own burden,' but, since we are also told to bear one another's burdens, and that it is more blessed to give than to receive, I must believe there are cases where it is right, yes, even a duty, to accept some assistance from those who give freely and gladly, and from their abundance, as I know Cousin Horace does."

"Well, I must try not to be so selfish as to grudge him his blessedness," remarked Mildred, playfully, though tears still shone in her eyes. "But, mother, how are you to do without me?"

"Oh, very nicely! Zillah and Ada are growing very helpful, Annie is no longer a mere baby, and—why, there is Celestia Ann!" she exclaimed joyously, suddenly breaking off her sentence, as a casual glance through a window showed her the tall, muscular figure of their former and most efficient maid-of-all-work coming in at the gate.

"Oh! if she has only come to stay, I shall feel as if I can be spared," cried Mildred, "Mother, how strangely difficulties are being taken out of the way."

Chapter Second.

" 'Tis you alone can save, or give my doom."
—OVID.

CELESTIA ANN had come to stay if wanted, of which in her secret soul she had no doubt; want of self-appreciation not being one of her failings—she knew her own value quite as well as did any one else.

"If you've got a girl, and don't want me," she remarked, upon announcing her errand, "it don't make no difference; I'm not perticler about workin' out this fall; if I was there's places enough; though I am free to own I feel a leetle more at home here than anywheres else, and set great store by you all."

"We have a girl," said Mrs. Keith, "but she leaves us in another week, and in the meanwhile, I shall be glad to have two, as Mildred and I will be very busy with the preparations for her journey."

"Journey! is she goin' off? 'taint on her weddin' trip, is it? I heerd there was talk of her gettin' married, and I said then I was bound to have a finger in that pie—makin' the weddin' cake."

"Oh, no, she's quite too young for that yet, Mrs. Keith said, with a slight smile, "she's only going South on a visit to some relations."

"And I want you to promise to stay and take care of mother till I come back, Celestia Ann," added Mildred.

"Well, you've got to promise first that you'll not stay forever," prudently stipulated Miss Hunsinger. "When do you 'low to come back?"

"Next spring."

"H'm! well, I don't mind engagin' for that length of time, provided my folks at home keeps well, so's I'm not needed there."

"Then it's a bargain?" queried Mildred joyously.

"Yes, I reckon."

And Celestia Ann hung up her sun-bonnet behind the kitchen door, and set to work at once with her wonted energy, while Mrs. Keith and Mildred withdrew to the bedroom of the latter to examine into the condition of her wardrobe, and consult as to needed repairs and additions.

They quickly decided that no new dresses should be purchased, and very little shopping of any kind done until her arrival in Philadelphia, as she could of course buy to much better advantage there, and learn what were the prevailing fashions, before having the goods made up.

Mrs. Keith had never made dress a matter of primary importance with herself or with her children, yet thought it well enough to conform to the fashions sufficiently to avoid being conspicuous for singularity of attire.

"We must give thought enough to the matter to decide how our clothes are to be made," she said, "and it is easier to follow the prevailing style than to contrive something different for ourselves ; provided it be pretty and becoming ; for I think it a duty we owe our friends to look as well as we can."

And on this principle she was desirous that Mildred's dress should be entirely suitable to her age and station, handsome and fashionable enough to ensure her against being an eyesore and annoyance to Mrs. Dinsmore, whose guest she was to be.

"The fashions are so slow in reaching these western towns that I know we must be at least a year or two behind," she remarked in a lively tone, as she turned over and examined Mildred's best dress—a pretty blue black silk, almost as good as new. "That doesn't trouble me so long as we are at home; but I don't want you to look outré to our relations and their friends, because that would be a mortification to them as well as to yourself. So though this is perfectly good, I think it will be best to try to match it and have it remodeled."

"Mother," said Mildred, "when it comes to buying dresses for myself how I shall miss you! I'm afraid I shall make some sad mistakes."

The young girl looked really troubled and anxious as she spoke and her mother answered in a kindly reassuring tone,

"I am not afraid to trust to your taste or judgment, so you need not be."

"But I shall not know where to go to find what I want, or whether the price asked is a fair one."

"Well, my dear child, even these trifling cares and anxieties we may carry to our kind heavenly Father, feeling sure that so a way will be provided out of the difficulty. Probably your aunt or uncle, or some other friend, will go with you."

The mother's tone was so cheerful and confident that Mildred caught her spirit and

grew gay and light-hearted over her preparations.

Although the dressmaking was deferred,
there was still enough to be done in the few
days of the allotted time, to keep both mother
and daughter very busy; which was just as
well, as it left them no leisure to grieve over
the approaching separation.

The news that she was going so far away
and to be absent so long, created some consternation in the little coterie to which Mildred
belonged

Claudina Chetwood and Lu Grange declared
themselves almost inconsolable, while Wallace
Ormsby was privately of the opinion that their
loss was as nothing compared to his.

Months ago he had decided that life would
be a desert without Mildred to share it with
him; but he had never found courage to tell
her so, for he feared the feeling was not recip-
rocated—that she had only a friendly liking
for him.

He had hoped to win her heart in time,
but now the opportunity was to be taken from
him and given to others. It was not a cheerful
prospect; and Mildred was so busy there seemed
no chance of getting a word alone with her.

" My mother tells me you are going away,

Mildred, on a long journey and for a lengthened stay?" Mr. Lord remarked inquiringly, and with a regretful tone in his voice, as he shook hands with her after the weekly evening service.

He had been absent from town for a week or two.

"Yes," she returned gayly, putting aside with determination the thought of the partings that must wrench her heart at the last. "I am all ready, trunk packed and everything, and expect to start to-morrow morning."

"Ah, it's unfortunate. We shall miss you sadly. May I—"

But some one called to him from the other side of the room; he was obliged to turn away without finishing his sentence, and Wallace Ormsby seized the opportunity to step up and offer his arm to Mildred.

She accepted it and they walked on in silence till they were quite out of earshot of the rest of the congregation.

Then Wallace opened his lips to speak, but the words he wanted would not come; he could only stammer out a trite remark about the weather.

"Yes; it's beautiful," said Mildred. "I do hope it will last so, at least till we reach the Wabash. However, we go in a covered vehicle, and I suppose will not get wet even if it should rain."

"I wish you weren't going!" cried Wallace impetuously. "No, not that either; for I think, I hope, the journey will do you good: but—O Mildred, I cannot bear the thought that you may—that somebody else will win you away from me. 1—I don't presume to say that I have any right, but I love you dearly, and always shall, and I do think I could make you happy if you only could return it," he went on speaking fast, now that he had found his tongue: "O Mildred, do you think you could?"

"I don't know, Wallace," she said, her voice trembling a little; "I have a very great respect and esteem for you, affection too," she added with some hesitation, and feeling the hot blood surge over her face at the words, "but I don't think it's quite the sort you want."

"You love somebody else?" he whispered hoarsely.

"No, no: there is no one I like better than I do you.   But we are both very young and—"

"Perhaps you might learn to like me in time?" he queried eagerly, tremulously, as one hoping even against hope.

"Yes: though I do *like* you now: but it ought to be something stronger, you know, and

I couldn't make any promises now, and neither must you."

"I should be glad to," he said, "for I am perfectly certain I should never repent."

He bade her good night at the gate, saying he would not make it good-bye if he might come to see her off in the morning.

"Certainly, Wallace," she said: "you are like one of the family; you have seemed that to all of us ever since your great kindness to us last summer."

"Don't speak of it," he answered hastily, "you conferred a great obligation in allowing me, for it was the greatest pleasure in life to be permitted to share your burdens."

Chapter Third.

"How poor a thing is pride!"—DANIEL.

THE parting was no slight trial to her who
went or those who stayed behind, particularly
the loving, tender mother. But both she and
Mildred bore it bravely, though the heart of
the latter almost failed her as she felt the clinging arms of the little ones about her neck, heard
their sobs and saw their tears; and again as she
found herself clasped to her father's and then to
her mother's breast with many a fond caress
and lowbreathed word of farewell and affection.

Wallace wrung her hand with a whispered
word of passionate entreaty, "O Mildred, darling, don't forget me! I'll remember you to the
day of my death."

The weather was fine, the air crisp, cool and
bracing, and when the town and a few miles of
prairie had been left behind, their way led
through woods beautiful with all the rich tints
of October's most lavish mood.

Mr. Dinsmore exerted himself to be entertaining and ere long he and Mildred were chat-
ting and laughing right merrily.

They took dinner at a farm house newly
built on a little clearing in the forest, finding
themselves not daintily served, but supplied with
an abundance of good, substantial, well cooked
food—bread, butter, coffee, ham and eggs, and
two or three kinds of vegetables, with stewed
dried apple pie for dessert.

After an hour's rest for themselves and
horses, they traveled on again, reaching a little
town in time to get their supper and night's
lodging at its tavern, where the fare and ac-
commodations were on a par with those of the
farm-house.

They had found the roads rough : those
they passed over the next day were worse still,
mostly corduroy, over the rounded logs of which
the wheels passed with constant jolting, and
where one had been displaced or rotted away,
as was occasionally the case, there would be a
sudden descent of, first the fore then the hind
wheels, with a violent jerk that nearly, or quite
threw them from their seats.

They reached Delphi on the Wabash, where
they were to take a steamboat, sore, weary and
very glad to make the change.

A night at the Delphi hotel, and the next morning they went aboard the boat which carried them down the Wabash and up the Ohio to Madison ; where they landed again and passed part of a day and night.   Embarking once more in a larger craft, they continued on their way up the Ohio as far as Portsmouth, whence a stage carried them across the country to Lansdale.

Miss Stanhope had not received the letter which should have informed her of their coming.   She was sitting alone by the fire, quietly knitting and thinking, perchance of the dear ones far away in Pleasant Plains, when the loud and prolonged " Toot! toot!" of a horn, followed by the roll and rumble of wheels, aroused her from her reverie.

" The evening stage," she said half-aloud, then rose hastily, dropped her knitting, and hurried to the door ; for surely it had stopped at her gate.

Yes, there it was ; a gentleman had alighted and was handing out a lady, while the guard was at the boot getting out their trunks.   She could see it all plainly by the moonlight, as she threw the door wide open.

" Who can they be ? " she asked herself, as she stepped quickly across the porch and down the garden path, to meet and welcome her un-expected guests.

The next moment Mildred's arms were about her neck and both were weeping for joy.

"Dear child, this is a glad surprise!" cried Miss Stanhope, straining the young girl to her breast. "But where are the rest?"

"Here; I'm the only one, Sister Wealthy," said Mr. Dinsmore, lifting his hat with one hand, while the other one was held out to her. "Haven't you a word of welcome for me?"

"Arthur Dinsmore, my brother-in-law!" she cried, taking the hand and offering him her lips. "I was never more surprised or delighted!

"Come in, come in, both of you. You must be cold, tired and hungry. I hope you've come to make a long stay. Simon will carry in the trunks," she went on rapidly as she seized Mildred's hand and led the way to the house, half beside herself with the sudden delight of seeing them.

She had many questions to ask, but the comfort of the weary travelers was the first thing to be attended to. She removed Mildred's wraps with her own hands, rejoicing over her the while as a mother might over a lost child restored, and would have done the same by Mr. Dinsmore if he had waited for her.

She soon had each cosily seated in a comfortable armchair beside the blazing fire, Simon kindling fires in the spare rooms, and Phillis in the kitchen, preparing a tempting meal.

"You couldn't be more welcome than you are, brother, or you Mildred, my dear child," she said, coming back from overseeing all these matters, "but you might have fared rather better, perhaps, if you had sent me word that you were coming."

"I wrote from Pleasant Plains," he answered. "The letter has been either lost or delayed in the mails."

"Ah well, we won't fret about it," she responded cheerily. "I at least am far too happy to fret about anything," she added, feasting her eyes upon Mildred's face.

"Dear child, you are worn and thin!" she exclaimed presently, her eyes filling, "that nursing was far too hard for you. How I wish I could have saved you from some of it! But you have come to stay all winter with me and have a good rest, haven't you?"

"No, no, she belongs to me for the winter," interposed Mr. Dinsmore, before Mildred could open her lips to reply. "If you want her company, Sister Wealthy, you must even make up your mind to be our guest also. What is to hinder you from shutting up your house and going with us to Roselands? I am sure I need not say that we would be delighted to have you do so."

"You are very kind, brother," she said, giving him an affectionate look, "but there are reasons why it would not do for me to leave home for so long a visit. Where is Horace? My dear sister Eva's son. I wish he had come with you. Poor boy!" and she sighed deeply.

A slight frown gathered on Mr. Dinsmore's brow at that. "He is hardly a subject for pity," he remarked, "he has just sailed for Europe with pleasant prospects before him and in apparently excellent spirits."

He looked fixedly at her, then glanced at Mildred, and taking the hint, she dropped the subject for that time.

She was at no loss for topics of conversation, so eager was she to learn all that could be told her in regard to the dear ones Mildred had left behind. Also she felt a lively interest in the family at Roselands, though they were not actually related to her, being the children of the present Mrs. Dinsmore, who was the second wife and successor to Horace's mother.

But finding herself alone with Mr. Dinsmore the next day, Miss Stanhope said, "You
tell me Horace has gone to Europe?   Will he
be long absent?"

"It is quite uncertain," he answered care-
lessly, "he may prolong his stay to a year or
more."

"He has his child with him, I hope."

"His child!"

Mr. Dinsmore seemed much annoyed.

"Certainly not," he said after a moment's
disturbed pause; "what could he do with her?
But I really hoped you knew nothing about
that ridiculous affair.   Pray how did you learn
it?"

"Horace told Marcia and requested her to
write the particulars to me," Aunt Wealthy
answered meekly.   "And she is still with her
guardian—poor little dear?"

"Yes, and will be I trust for years to come.
That mad escapade of Horace's—for I can call
his hasty, ill-timed, imprudent marriage by no
other name—has been to me a source of untold
mortification and annoyance."

"It was not a bad match except on account
of their extreme youth?" Miss Stanhope said
in a tone between assertion and inquiry.

"I consider it so most decidedly," he returned, his eyes kindling with anger. "Elsie Grayson, the daughter of a man who, though wealthy, has made all his money by trade, was no fit match for my son, and I consider it a fortunate thing that she did not live: it would have been, in my estimation, still more fortunate if her child had died with her."

Miss Stanhope was shocked.

" O Arthur, how can you ! " she exclaimed, tears starting to her eyes, " how can you feel so toward your own little granddaughter ; a poor motherless baby too ! Truly pride must be a great hardener of the heart."

"Old Grayson's grandchild," he muttered, rising to pace the floor in a hasty excited manner." Please oblige me by not mentioning this subject again," he said : " it is exceedingly unpleasant to me."

Miss Stanhope sighed inwardly.

" Arthur," she said, " Pride goeth before destruction, and an haughty spirit before a fall."

She did not broach the subject again during the remainder of his brief stay with her.

" I am going out for a look at your town," he said, taking up his hat. "I hope," turning back at the door, with his hand on the knob, " that Mildred has heard nothing of this affair ? " he remarked inquiringly.

"She knows all that I do, I believe," Miss Stanhope answered quietly. "It seemed to be Horace's wish that she should be told."

Mr. Dinsmore went out with a groan, and Mildred coming in at that instant by another door, heard, and inquired somewhat anxiously, of her aunt, what was the matter.

Miss Stanhope thought it best to tell her and advise avoidance of any allusion to Horace's wife or child, when in her uncle's presence; unless he should himself take the initiative.

Mildred promised to be careful, "Though why he should feel so I cannot understand,' she added, "I, for my part, feel the greatest interest in that little child, and regret exceedingly that I shall not see her. But Cousin Horace's feelings toward her are more inexplicable still. How can he help loving his own little baby girl, who seems to have no one else to love and cherish her except the servants!"

It was now an hour since they had left the breakfast table: Miss Stanhope's morning duties connected with the care of the household, had been attended to, Phillis and Simon had received their orders for the day, and the good lady might conscientiously indulge herself and Mildred in the lengthened chat both had been longing for ever since the arrival of the latter the previous night.

Of course the first and most absorbingly
interesting topic was the home circle at Pleasant Plains. That thoroughly discussed, they
passed on to friends and neighbors both there
and here, each finding numerous questions to
ask the other, and many a bit of news to give.

"What has become of poor Mrs. Osborne
and Frank?" Mildred inquired.

"Ah, she has gone home at last, and is forever done with pain and sickness," Miss Stanhope answered. "It was hard for Frank, but
a blessed release to her—poor dear woman! It
was three weeks ago she went, and a week after
Frank came to bid me good-bye. He's going
to work his way through college, he told me,
and make his mark in the world. And, Milly,
my dear," she added with a slightly mischievous smile, "he hinted pretty broadly that when
his laurels were won they would be laid at the
feet of a certain young girl of my acquaintance;
if I thought there might be some faint hope
that she would not deem it presumption."

"And what did you answer to that, Aunt
Wealthy;" queried Mildred, with heightened
color and a look of mingled vexation and amusement. "He is such a mere boy!" she added,
"I never thought of him as anything else."

"Of course not; nor did I. But he is a

good, true, noble fellow, bright and intelligent
above the ordinary, and very modest and unas-
suming with it all.   He will make a fine
man."

"Yes, I think so too, and if he happens to
fancy one of my younger sisters, I'll consent
with all my heart, and do what I can to further
his suit."

Aunt Wealthy shook her head and smiled.
"It's not what he wants now; but who
knows?   Time does work wonderful changes
now and then."

Mildred's thoughts seemed to have wan
dered away from the subject; she was silent
for a moment; then suddenly asked, "Aunt
Wealthy, do you know what sort of person—
Dear me, what am I to call her?   Mrs. or
Aunt Dinsmore?   What would you do about
it?"

"I should ask her what title she preferred,
and act accordingly.   No; I have never met
her, and know very little about her, except
that she is not a pious woman."

"And uncle?"

"Is not a Christian either," Miss Stanhope
said sorrowfully, as Mildred paused, leaving
her sentence unfinished; "believes nothing
more necessary to secure salvation than an

honest, upright, moral life. My dear child, you are going into an atmosphere of worldliness, and will need to watch and pray, keeping close to the Master. Ah! what joy that we need never be any farther away from him in one place than another!"

"Yes, that was what mother said," murmured Mildred, tears filling her eyes at the thought of the many miles now lying between her and that loved parent and friend; "she promised to pray daily for me that I might be kept from the evil, and you will do so, too, Aunt Wealthy, will you not?"

"Indeed I will, dear child," was the earnest response.

Chapter Fourth.

"Wear this for me."—SHAKESPEARE.

"YOUR traveling suit is very neat and becoming—very ladylike," Miss Stanhope remarked, with an approving glance at Mildred's trim figure, "I don't think your Uncle Dinsmore can have felt that he had any reason to be ashamed of you."

"I hope not," was the smiling rejoinder, "and I did not see any indications of it."

"But how about the rest of your wardrobe, child? I fear you had small choice of material in Pleasant Plains, and very little time for making up your purchases. We might do rather better here, if we could persuade your uncle to lengthen his intended stay."

"Thank you, auntie dear, you are always so kind and thoughtful," Mildred said, "but I don't think he could be persuaded, and indeed I should not like to have him delay for my sake, because I know he and his wife are anxious to get home before the cold weather sets in.'

She went on to explain her plans, and to tell of her Cousin Horace's generous gift.

"That was just like him, he's an open-handed, noble fellow," was Aunt Wealthy's comment, "you need never hesitate to take a kindness from him, because he enjoys it, and is abundantly able. But I must not be outdone by him," she continued with a smile, rising and going to her bureau—for they were in her bedroom now—"or rather, I wish to do my share in proportion to my ability."

Mildred protested that her wants were already well supplied; but playfully bidding her be quiet and let older and wiser heads judge of that, Miss Stanhope proceeded to take a key from her pocket, unlock the drawers of her bureau, and bring forth her treasures:—a quantity of rich old lace, that the finest lady in the land might have been proud to wear, several handsome rings, a diamond pin, and a beautiful gold chain for the neck.

"They are old fashioned, dearie," she said, " but n. one will mistake them for pinchbeck and colored glass," she added, with her low, musical laugh, as she threw the chain about

Mildred's neck, and slipped the rings upon her fingers.

The girl's cheeks flushed, and her eyes sparkled.

"O, Aunt Wealthy," she cried, "how can you trust such treasures to my keeping? Old fashioned indeed! They are all the more delightful for that, as showing that one does not belong to the mushroom gentry, but to a good, substantial old family. But you must not let me use them, lest they should be lost or stolen. I should be frightened out of my wits in either case."

"Nonsense, child! You would have no need; for the loss would be more yours than mine; I shall never wear them again, and they will all belong, some day, to you or your sisters," Miss Stanhope said, turning to her bureau once more.

Lifting out something carefully wrapped in a towel, she laid it in Mildred's lap, saying, "This, too, you must take with you. You will want a handsome wrap in Philadelphia, before you can go out to buy, and this will answer the purpose even better than anything you would feel able to purchase. Won't it?" she queried with another of her sweet, silvery laughs.

Mildred fairly caught her breath in delighted surprise.

"O Aunt Wealthy! your beautiful India shawl! you can't mean to lend *that* to me!"

"That is just what I mean, Milly; stand up a minute, dear," she answered gayly, taking it from its wrappings and draping it about the slender girlish figure. "There! nothing could be more becoming. I can only lend, not give it, because it is already willed to your mother. But it is to descend always to the eldest daughter."

"Aunt Wealthy, I'm afraid to borrow it; afraid something might happen to it. So please put it away again."

"Tut, child! something might happen to it at home. Suppose the house should burn down with everything in it; wouldn't I be glad the shawl was saved by being far away in your keeping?"

It was very rich and costly, and highly prized by Miss Stanhope as the gift of a favorite brother, long since dead. He had been a wanderer, lived many years in China and India, whence he had sent her, from time to time, rare and beautiful things, of which this was one, then at length he came home to die in her arms, leaving her the bulk of his fortune enough to make her very comfortable.

Her means were ample for her own needs, but not for her abundant charities; for she spent little on herself, but gave with a literal hand.

"Yes, I know you would, auntie," Mildred said, passing her hand caressingly over the soft, rich folds; "but in my wildest dreams I never supposed you would lend this to me. And if I were in your place I don't think I'd do it," she concluded with an arch look and smile.

"You are a careful little body and I'm not afraid to trust you. You must carry it with you, my child, and wear it too; as a favor to me; for you can't suppose I feel willing to have Mrs. Dinsmore's aristocratic nose turn up at niece of mine for lack of a little finery that lies idle in my bureau drawer?"

"Ah, if you put it on that score I can't refuse," laughed Mildred, her face sparkling with pleasure, "and oh, but you're good to let me have it! It is so handsome, auntie! it seems like a whole outfit in itself," she went on, dancing about the room in almost wild delight.

Then sobering down a little and standing before the glass to note the effect, "I don't think," she said, "that I had seen it over half a dozen times before—when worn on some grand occasion by you or mother—and it has always inspired me with a kind of awe, as something to be looked at from a respectful distance and by no means handled. So it seems almost beyond belief that I am actually to wear it."

The few days Mr. Dinsmore had apportioned to their visit to Lansdale flew rapidly by; all too rapidly for Miss Stanhope, who was loath to part with them, Mildred especially; but the young girl, full of youthful eagerness to see the world, was hardly sorry to go, spite of her sincere affection for her aunt.

They returned to the Ohio River as they had come, striking it at the nearest point, where they once more embarked in a steamboat; taking passage for Pittsburgh.

They were again favored with pleasant weather, for the most of the time, and Mildred enjoyed the trip. Mr. Dinsmore was very kind and attentive to her comfort, and she made some agreeable acquaintances among her fellow passengers.

They dined and spent some hours at a hotel in Pittsburgh, then took the cars for Philadelphia.

It was a new mode of travel to Mildred, and not what she would have chosen; she had read newspaper accounts of railroad accidents, and felt in going upon the train, that she was risking life and limb

But she kept her fears to herself, determined not to be an annoyance to her uncle, and he never suspected how her heart was quaking as she took quiet possession of the seat he selected for her.

" We are early," he remarked with a glance about the almost empty car, as he sat down beside her; then looking at his watch, " Yes, fully fifteen minutes to wait before the train starts. Well, that's a good deal better than being too late.

"Mildred, there's something I want to say to you before we join your aunt, and perhaps this is as good a time for it as any. There! don't *l* e alarmed," as she gave him a startled look, ' it's nothing unpleasant; only that I would rather you would not say anything to Mrs. Dinsmore about your father's circumstances. My dear, I am not meaning to wound your feelings," he added hastily, for she was blushing painfully and her eyes had filled.

" l think quite as much of him, and of you all as if you were rolling in wealth. But my wife is—well, does not always see things precisely as I do, and it will make us more comfortable all round if she is left to suppose that your mother is still in possession of the fortune she once had."

He paused and Mildred, understanding that some answer was expected from her, said, a little tremulously, for she was hurt, "I cannot act a lie, Uncle Dinsmore, and poverty ought not to be considered a disgrace."

"Of course it shouldn't and I am not asking you to practice deceit any more than just to keep things to yourself which others have no right to pry into. It need not be difficult; for Mrs. Dinsmore is not one of the prying kind; and Horace and I will regard it as a favor to us, if you will simply leave it to me to take care of your expenses without question or remark."

This last was spoken with such winning kindness of tone and manner that even Mildred's pride was disarmed: grateful tears shone in her eyes as she turned them upon him.

"My dear good uncle," she whispered, laying her hand upon his with a gesture of confiding affection, "I don't know how to thank you and Cousin Horace, and I cannot refuse to do as you wish, but indeed you must not let me be any more expense to you than if I were but an ordinary guest; instead of the extraordinary one I am," she added, laughing to hide her emotion.

"I shall have my own way about it, you may depend, whatever that may chance to be," he answered with mock severity of tone.

Mildred laughed again, this time a really mirthful, happy laugh; feeling her heart grow strangely light.

After all she could not help being glad that Mrs. Dinsmore was not to know their comparative poverty; that she herself was not to be looked upon as a poor relation who might be snubbed at pleasure and perhaps twitted with her lack of means: or worse still, treated with lofty, or with pitying condescension.

"Yes," Mr. Dinsmore went on, half to himself, half to her, "wealth is but a secondary matter after all; family is the main thing. I believe in blood, and want nothing to do with your parvenu aristocracy, be they never so rich. Well what say you, my dear?" for Mildred's face had grown very thoughtful.

"I'm afraid I am naturally inclined to think just so, but—"

"Well, are not my views correct and proper?" he asked good humoredly, as she paused with a look of some confusion.

"Is not character what we should look at, rather than anything else?" she modestly inquired, "is not true nobility that of the heart and life? It is what father and mother have taught me, and I think, too, is most consistent with the teachings of God's word."

At that moment there was a sudden and large influx of passengers, some of them talking noisily and her query remained unanswered.

Chapter Fifth.

"Walk
Boldly and wisely in that light thou hast.
There is a hand above will help thee on."
—BIRLEY'S FESTUS.

"WELL, my dear, what do you think of her?" asked Mr. Dinsmore, addressing his wife.

Mildred had just left the room to don bonnet and shawl preparatory to a shopping expedition. She and her uncle had arrived in Philadelphia late the previous night, and Mrs. Dinsmore and the children having already retired, Mildred's first sight of them had been at the breakfast table this morning;—the meal being partaken of in the private parlor belonging to the suite of apartments the Dinsmores were occupying in one of the best hotels of the city.

"I am agreeably disappointed, I must confess," Mrs. Dinsmore replied to her husband's query. "She is decidedly pretty and extremely ladylike in manner and appearance. Even her dress,—though not quite in the fashion—bespeaks her a person of taste and refinement, In fact I think I shall enjoy playing chaperone to her and introducing her to our friends at the South."

" Ah, I thought you could not fail to be pleased with her," Mr. Dinsmore said, looking much gratified, "and I knew you were when you bade her call you aunt. I imagine she had been a little troubled to decide just how she was to address you."

"Well, since I find she is not the sort one need feel ashamed of, I've no objection to her claiming relationship, though there is none at all in point of fact; but if she had proved the awkward, ungainly, uncouth girl I expected, I should have requested her to call me Mrs. Dinsmore," remarked that lady languidly. "I wonder if she has much shopping to do? I hope not, for I really do not feel equal to the exertion of assisting her."

" Driving about in a carriage and sitting in the stores; I should not think it need be so very fatiguing," remarked her husband.

"Of course not, Mr. Dinsmore; men never do see why anything should fatigue their wives," she retorted with some petulance.

"Then Miss Worth and I will have to manage it between us. You expect her to-day, do you not?'

"She was to come to-day; but of course she won't. People never do as they promise. The fact is she oughtn't to have gone at all, leaving me here alone with servants and children; so selfish and inconsiderate!"

"But, my dear, it would have been very hard for her to go back without having spent a short time with her family."

"And her pleasure is to be considered before my comfort, of course."

"Really, I had hoped your comfort had not been neglected," Mr. Dinsmore said, in a tone of some irritation, as he glanced from the richly attired figure in the easy chair, opposite his own, to the luxurious appointments of the room; "what more can you wish?"

The entrance of Mrs. Dinsmore's maid, bringing her bonnet and shawl, saved the lady the necessity of replying to the somewhat inconvenient query, and her husband turned to the morning paper.

Then Mildred came in.

Mrs. Dinsmore, standing before the pier glass, saw the girl's figure reflected there, and the latter could not help enjoying her start of surprise.

"What an elegant shawl!" she exclaimed, turning hastily about to take a better view, "real India! You needn't be ashamed to show yourself anywhere in that! Though your bonnet is quite out of date, as you warned me," she added by way of preventing too great elation from her praise of the shawl.

"No matter," interposed Mr. Dinsmore, throwing down his paper, "we'll soon set that right. The carriage is waiting. Are any of the children going?"

"Yes, Adelaide, Louise and Lora. Mammy and Fanny have taken the younger ones out."

The three little girls came in at the moment. They were gayly and expensively dressed, in the height of the fashion. They looked curiously at Mildred, then Louise, the second in age, a child of ten, whispered to her mother,

"What a fright of a bonnet, it's not in the style at all, and I don't want her along if she's going to wear that."

"Hush! it's no matter," returned the mother in the same low key, "she won't be seen in the carriage, and we'll drive directly to Mrs. Brown's, and get her a handsome one."

"Oh! what a pretty shawl, cousin," exclaimed Adelaide, "real India, isn't it? Come on, mamma, and all of you," she added, hurrying into the hall, "it's time we were off."

"Adelaide always wants to direct the rest of us," complained Louise, "I wish, mamma, you'd make her know her place."

"Tut, tut! remember she's three years older than you. But if you children are going to quarrel, you must stay behind," said Mr. Dinsmore, standing back to let his wife and Mildred pass out first.

"No, no, papa, that won't do, because we're to be fitted with hats and shoes," laughed the youngest of the three, putting her hand into his, "besides, I didn't quarrel."

"That's true enough, Lora," he answered, leading her down the stairs, "and in fact, I believe no one did but Louise, who is apt to be the complainer."

The drive to the milliner's was so short that Mildred thought they might as well have walked. She would have preferred it as giving her a better opportunity to see the city; but no; in that case she would have had to mortify her friends by an exhibition of her unfashionable head-gear.

The next half hour was spent in turning

over ribbons, flowers and feathers, discussing styles, and trying on bonnets.

At length one was found which pleased both Mrs. Dinsmore and Mildred, but the price asked seemed to the latter extravagant.

" Do you think I ought to go so high, Aunt ?" she asked in an undertone. " Is it worth it ?"

" I think the price reasonable, and the hat no finer than you ought to wear," returned Mrs. Dinsmore coldly.

Mildred, blushing, turned to the saleswoman, saying, " I will take it," and began counting out the money.

" Stay," said her aunt, " you will want a hat for travelling in."

A plainer and less expensive one was selected for that purpose, the handsome bonnet put on, the bill paid, and they returned to their carriage, Mildred feeling pleasantly conscious of her improved appearance, yet a trifle uneasy at the thought of how fast her money was melting away.

Their next visit was to a fashionable shoe store. Mrs. Dinsmore had the children and herself fitted with several pairs each, and by her advice, Mildred, too, bought slippers for the house, and heavy walking shoes.

"You must have, besides, a pair of gaiters to match each handsome dress you buy," Mrs. Dinsmore said to her as they re-entered the carriage.

That announcement filled Mildred with dismay. At this rate her purse would be emptied before the demands upon it were nearly satisfied. What was she to do? She had been eager to select her dresses, but now was thankful for the respite afforded her by Mrs. Dinsmore's declaration that she was too much fatigued for any more shopping, and that therefore they would return to their hotel.

"I'm going to lie down till it is time to dress for dinner, and would advise you to do the same," she said to Mildred as they re-entered their parlor, and our heroine retreated at once to her own room, glad of the opportunity to think over her perplexity in solitude, and ask guidance and help of her best Friend, who, as she rejoiced in knowing, was abundantly able and willing to help her in every time of need.

She cast her burden on Him, then threw herself on the bed, and being very weary with her long journey, soon fell asleep.

Two hours later she was roused by a knock at her door. She sprang up and opened it to find a porter there with an armful of brown paper parcels and a note for her.

"Is there not some mistake?" she asked in surprise.

"No, Miss: No. 95, and here's the name on the note and the bundles."

"Why yes, it is my name, sure enough!" she exclaimed. "Well, you may bring them in."

The man laid the packages down and departed, while Mildred, only waiting to close the door after him, tore open the note.

"My dear niece," so it ran, "you must please excuse the liberty I have taken in selecting your dresses for you. Your Aunt Wealthy put some money into my hands to be laid out for you. The letter containing her remittance and also one from Roselands which hurries us home, came to hand a few minutes after you and Mrs. Dinsmore had left the hotel. Miss Worth arrived while I was in the act of reading them, and with her assistance I ventured to do your shopping for you. The contents of the parcels sent with this are the result.

"Hoping they may suit your taste, I am your affectionate uncle, A. D."

For some minutes after the note had been hastily read and laid aside, Mildred's fingers

were very busy with twine and wrapping
paper, bringing to light beautiful and costly
things, while her cheeks burned with excitement and her eyes danced with delight, or
filled with tears of mingled pleasure and pain.

She could not fail to rejoice in such wealth
of lovely things, yet it hurt her pride of independence that she must take them as gifts; and
that from one who was scarcely related to her,
for well she knew that Mr. Dinsmore must have
paid a large proportion of the price from his
own purse.   There were materials for three
beautiful evening dresses, a sage colored merino,
fine and soft, an all wool delaine—royal purple
with an embroidered sprig; also three silks—a
black, a dark brown, and a silver grey; each
rich and heavy enough to almost stand alone,
and there was a box of kid gloves; one or two
pairs to match each dress, the rest white for
evening wear.   Nor had suitable trimmings for
the dresses been forgotten: they were there in
beautiful variety—ribbons, buttons, heavy silk
fringes; nothing had been overlooked.

Mildred seemed to herself to be in a dream
she could hardly believe that such riches were
really here.

But there came a rap at the door and opening she found Mr. Dinsmore standing there.

"May I come in?" he asked with grave cheerfulness.

She stepped back silently, her heart too full for speech, and passing in he closed the door.

"My dear child, you will excuse me?" he began, but throwing her arms round his neck she burst into tears.

"O, uncle, you are so kind! but it is too much," she sobbed, hiding her face on his shoulder.

"Nonsense! the merest trifle!" he said, stroking her hair. "But if you don't like them—"

"Like them!" she cried. "They're just lovely! every one of them, but—"

"No, no! no buts," he said gayly; "if they suit your taste it's all right. The gaiters that Mrs. Dinsmore says are necessary to match the dresses, can be made nearer home and we'll have two days, Friday and Saturday for sight seeing. This is Thursday, and early Monday morning we leave for Roselands."

"But O, uncle, you shouldn't have spent so much money on me,' began Mildred.

"I, child? your Aunt Wealthy you mean Didn't you read my note?"

"Yes sir; and I know I must thank her for a part, but only a part of these beautiful things.

"Dear me, how very wise we are," he said jocosely and chucking her playfully under the chin; "yet perhaps not quite so wise as we think. Now if you want to do me a favor, just call to mind our talk in the cars the other day, and say no more about this.

"Mrs. Dinsmore and Miss Worth know nothing but that I had money of yours in my hands and have used it in doing your shopping for you ; and it is decidedly my wish that they neither know nor suspect anything further. Will you oblige me by being quiet about it?"

"I would do anything I possibly could to oblige you, Uncle Dinsmore," she answered, looking into his eyes with hers full of grateful tears.

"Ah, that's my good girl," he said, "Now dry your eyes and we'll go down to dinner. It is to be served for the family in our own parlor, and is probably on the table now."

Dinner was on the table, and as they entered the family were in the act of taking their places about it.

Miss Worth the governess was with them. She was an intelligent looking, but rather plain featured woman of perhaps thirty-five. Her manners were unobtrusive, she was very quiet and reserved, seemingly self-absorbed.

Mildred's first impressions were not too favorable. The thought in the girl's mind was, " she's a disagreeable old maid, and I'm sure I shall never like her."

Yet the face, though slightly sad and care-worn when at rest, would by many have been preferred to Mrs. Dinsmore's in its faded beauty, and listless or fretful and annoyed expression.

The bright, fresh young faces of the children pleased Mildred better than either. There were six of them in all; Arthur, Walter, and Enna were all younger than the three little girls whose acquaintance she had made in the morning—the last named a mere baby. They were pretty children and not ill-behaved considering that they had been used to an almost unlimited amount of petting and indulgence.

"Miss Worth has been telling me about your dresses, Mildred," remarked Mrs. Dinsmore, "I hope you will like them; I should think from her description, they must be very handsome."

" They are, *very*," Mildred answered, with a vivid blush. "I don't think I could possibly have been better suited." And turning to Miss Worth, she thanked her warmly for the trouble she had taken in her behalf.

"It was no trouble, and you are heartily

welcome, Miss Keith," returned the governess, a smile lighting up her features into positive comeliness.

Mr. Dinsmore changed the subject, by a proposal to take his wife and Mildred to some place of amusement for the evening.

"How thoughtless you are, my dear," said Mrs. Dinsmore, "I am sure Mildred must be too much fatigued by her journey to think of going out."

"I doubt it," he returned, laughing. "What do you say, Milly?"

"That I don't think I am," she answered brightly, "a two hours' nap this afternoon having refreshed me wonderfully."

"Then we'll go," he said, "there's an opportunity to hear some fine music, and I don't want to miss it. You will go with us, Mrs. Dinsmore?"

"No," she said coldly, "I do not feel equal to the exertion."

She was not an invalid, but had barely escaped becoming such through extreme aversion to exercise of body or mind.

Mr. Dinsmore then extended his invitation to Miss Worth, overruled her objection, that she feared the children would require her attention, by saying that the servants would give

them all the care they needed, and insisted
upon her acceptance, unless she, too, must plead
fatigue as an excuse for declining.

Before the governess had time to open her
lips in reply, Mrs. Dinsmore suddenly announced that she had changed her mind; she
would go, and really she could not feel easy
about the children, unless Miss Worth were
there to see that they were properly attended to.

It was a disappointment to the latter, who
seldom enjoyed such a treat, but she quietly
acquiesced, sighing inwardly, but giving no
outward sign.

"Shall we walk or ride?" queried Mr.
Dinsmore, looking at Mildred. "The distance
is about four squares."

"Oh, let us walk," she was about to exclaim, feeling an eager desire for the exercise,
and to look at the buildings and brightly
lighted windows; but Mrs. Dinsmore decided
this question also with an emphatic,

"We will take a carriage of course. What
can you be thinking of, Mr. Dinsmore?"

They had left the table and Mildred was
considering how she should excuse herself, that
she might retire to her own room and finish a
letter to her mother, when Mrs. Dinsmore
said, "You must show me your pretty things

now, Mildred. There il be plenty of time before we have to dress for the concert."

" Dress !" echoed Mildred in dismay, " really Aunt, I have nothing more suitable to wear than this I have on," glancing down at the blue black silk she had been wearing all that day.

" What matter ? that's neat fitting and handsome enough for any occasion," interrupted Mr. Dinsmore.

" It will do very well, if you don't throw back your shawl," remarked his wife, glancing askance at the really neat, ladylike and pretty dress.

" The place will be crowded and warm," said Mr. Dinsmore, " and if you find your shawl burdensome, Mildred, you are to throw it back and be comfortable." His wife gave him an indignant glance.

" She can take a fan," she said shortly, " I'll lend her one that I'll not be ashamed to see her carry."

Mildred was glad she could say she had a pretty fan of her own, and would not need to borrow, and with it said she would doubtless be able to refrain from throwing back her shawl in a way to exhibit the unfashionable make of her dress.

Mrs. Dinsmore graciously condescended to approve of the purchases made by her husband and the governess, saying she really thought she hardly could have done better herself, and it was an immense relief to know that the thing was done without any worry or responsibility coming upon her, she was so ill able to bear such things.

On hearing which, our heroine felt unspeakably thankful that her assistance had not been asked.

Mildred enjoyed the concert extremely; also the sight-seeing, which with a little more shopping fully occupied the next two days, and the church-going of the day following. She found time before breakfast Saturday morning, for doing her packing and finishing the letter to her mother. On Monday morning there was little time for anything but breakfast before they must go on board the steamer which was to carry them to a seaport town within a few miles of Roselands.

Chapter Sixth.

"O'er the glad waters of the dark, blue sea."

BYRON.

IT was Mildred's first sight of the ocean. The November air was chill but the sun shone brightly, and well wrapped up, she found the deck not an uncomfortable place; so kept her station there all through the passage down the river and bay; though Mrs. Dinsmore very soon retreated, shivering, to the cabin, and called in nurses and children; with exception of Adelaide, who insisted upon remaining with her father and cousin, and was, as usual, allowed to have her own way.

"There, we have a full view of old ocean," Mr. Dinsmore said, as they steamed out of the bay. "You never saw anything like that before, Mildred?"

"Yes; the great lakes look very similar," she answered, gazing away over the restless waters, her eyes kindling with enthusiasm.

"How grandly beautiful it is! I think I should never weary of the sight and should like to live where I could watch it day by day in all its moods."

"Roselands is not so very far off from the coast," said Adelaide. "A ride of a few miles in one direction gives us a distant view."

"Oh, I am glad of that!" Mildred exclaimed.

"And we will place a pony and servant at your command, so that you can ride in that direction whenever you will," added Mr. Dinsmore.

Mildred took her eyes from the sea long enough to give him a look of delight that fully repaid him; nor did she spare words, but told him he was wonderfully kind to her.

"Tell about being on the lakes, cousin," pleaded Adelaide. "When was it and who was with you?"

There had been a little homesickness tugging at Mildred's heartstrings, and that last question brought the tears to her eyes and a tremble to her lips. She had a short struggle with herself before she could so command her voice as to speak quite steadily.

But when she had once begun it was not difficult to go on and give a circumstantial

account of their journey to Indiana: especially
as Adelaide proved a delighted and deeply
interested listener.

"Thank you," she said, when the story had
come to an end. "But do tell me more about
your brothers and sisters—everything you can
think of. What a lot of them there is! I
think Cyril and Don must be comical little
fellows."

"Yes; and very provokingly mischievous
at times," Mildred said, laughing at the recollection of some of their pranks, which she went
on to describe for Adelaide's entertainment.

But the sun had set and the air was so cold
that they were compelled to seek the shelter of
the cabin.

They found warmth and brightness there.
Mrs. Dinsmore was half reclining on a sofa,
her husband reading the evening paper by her
side.

"Well, I'm glad you've come in at last,"
she said, with a reproachful look directed at
Mildred. "It was really very thoughtless to
keep Adelaide out so late."

"She didn't keep me, mamma," answered
the child with spirit. "I could have come in
any minute if I had chosen. I was not even
asked to stay."

" Don't be pert, Adelaide," said her mother.
" Dear me, how the vessel begins to rock! I
shall be deathly sick before morning."

" That would have been less likely to happen if you had followed Mildred's example in
staying on deck as long as possible," remarked
her husband, turning his paper and beginning
another article.

" I should have caught my death of cold,"
she retorted snappishly, " but perhaps you
wouldn't have cared if I had. And I think it's
quite insulting to have a chit of a girl like that
held up to me as an example."

Mildred had walked away and did not hear
this last remark. Adelaide had slipped her hand
into Mildred's, and was saying, " I like you,
cousin. We'll be good friends, shan't we ? "

" It shall not be my fault if we're not,"
Mildred said, forcing a smile ; for Mrs. Dinsmore's fault-finding had hurt her feelings and
caused a decided increase of the homesickness.
But determined to overcome it she gathered
the children about her at a safe distance from
their mother, and told them stories till interrupted by the summons to the tea table.

They had a rather rough sea that night
and the next day, causing a good deal of sickness among the passengers. Mildred, taught

by past experience, fought bravely against it seeking the deck soon after sunrise and spending almost the whole day there in company with her uncle.

The second day she experienced no difficulty and was joined by her cousins; but Mrs. Dinsmore kept her berth to the end of the voyage, and when the vessel arrived in port, came from her stateroom pale, weak and disconsolate.

The last stage of the journey was made in carriages.

They reached Roselands just as the sun was setting amid a mass of crimson, gold and amber-colored clouds forming a gorgeous background to a landscape of more than ordinary beauty.

"Oh, how lovely!" exclaimed Mildred, as her uncle handed her from the carriage. "I was prepared to be charmed with the place, but it exceeds my expectations."

"Let me bid you welcome and hope that first impressions may prove lasting, your stay here most enjoyable," he said, with a gratified smile.

But now Mildred's attention was taken up by the reception that had been prepared for them :—just such an one as she had often heard described by her mother.

The plantation was large; the dwelling
also; and a dozen or more of house servants
headed by the housekeeper, who was a very
respectable white woman, had ranged themselves in a double row across the veranda, and
down the wide entrance hall.

Their faces were full of delight, their hands
held out in joyous greeting, glad words of welcome on every tongue, as master, mistress,
guest, and children, with their attendants,
passed slowly between the ranks, shaking hands
and making kind inquiries right and left.

Some of the older ones remembered Mildred's mother, and our heroine's heart warmed
toward them as they sounded " Miss Marcia's"
praises, and averred that her daughter bore a
striking resemblance to her in looks.

" Mrs. Brown, this young lady is my niece,"
said Mr. Dinsmore, laying a hand on Mildred's
shoulder, and addressing himself to the housekeeper, " and I commend her to your special
care. Please see that she is well waited upon,
and wants for nothing that house or plantation
can supply. Here, Rachel," to a young mu-
latto girl, " I appoint you Miss Mildred's waiting maid ; you are to be always at her call, and
do whatever she directs."

" Yes, massa," the girl answered, dropping

a deep courtesy first to him, then to Mildred
whom she regarded with a look of smiling approval, "dis chile berry glad ob de chance.
Shall I show de way to yo' room, now, miss?"
Mildred gave a smiling assent, and was immediately conducted to a spacious, elegantly furnished apartment, where an open wood fire
blazed and crackled, sending around a ruddy
light that rendered that of the wax candles in
the heavy, highly polished silver candlesticks
on the mantel, almost a superfluity.

Mildred sent a very satisfied, appreciative
glance about her, then turning to her young
handmaiden, who stood quietly awaiting her
orders, asked if there were time to change her
dress before tea.

"Yes, Miss, plenty time. Whar yo'
trunks, Miss? Oh! heyah dey come," slipping out of the way of two of the men servants as they entered with Mildred's luggage.

Mrs. Brown followed close in their rear,
bade them unstrap the trunks before leaving,
inquired of Mildred if there were anything
more she could do for her, and said she hoped
she would be very comfortable.

"Rachel is young and has not had much
experience in the duties of ladies' maid," she
added, "but I think you will find her trusty

and willing. Would you not like to have her unpack your things and arrange them in the bureau and wardrobe? Then the trunks can be put away out of sight till they are wanted again."

" Yes, that will be very nice," said Mildred, producing the keys. " But will there be time before tea?"

" Hardly, I'm afraid, Miss Keith, if you have any change to make in your dress; but later in the evening, if that will answer?"

" Oh, yes, quite as well."

Mrs. Brown took her departure, Mr. Dinsmore looked in for a moment to see that his young guest had not been neglected, and how she was pleased with her new quarters; then Mildred, left alone with her maid, opened a trunk, laid out the dress and ornaments she wished to wear, and proceeded with Rachel's assistance, to make a somewhat hurried toilet.

The tea-bell rang, and Adelaide's bright face peeped in at the door.

" Ready, cousin? I'll show you the way."

They entered the supper-room looking fresh and blooming as two roses.

Mr. Dinsmore assigned Mildred the seat of honor at his right hand, and complimented her on the becomingness of her attire.

She was the only guest, the children were all allowed to come to the table, and they were a merry family party, everybody rejoicing in being at home again after an absence of several months.

The table was loaded with delicacies, skillfully prepared; for old Phebe, the cook, was a real genius in the culinary art—the cloth was of finest damask, the service of rare china and costly silverware, and the attendance all that could be desired.

Pleading excessive fatigue, Mrs. Dinsmore retired to her own apartments immediately upon the conclusion of the meal.

"You look quite too fresh and bright to be thinking of bed yet," Mr. Dinsmore remarked, laying his hand affectionately on Mildred's shoulder; "will you come to the library with me?"

She gave a pleased assent and they were soon cosily seated on either side of the fire there, a table covered with books, papers and periodicals drawn up between them.

"How do you like this room?" Mr. Dinsmore asked.

"Oh, very much!" Mildred answered, sending a sweeping glance from side to side, noting all the attractions of the place, from the

rich Turkey carpet, handsome rugs, comfortable chairs, couches and tables, to the long lines
of well filled book shelves, statues, statuettes and
busts, and two or three fine paintings on the
walls.

"That is right," he said with a pleased
smile. "I want you to feel perfectly at home
here; coming in whenever you please and staying just as long as you like, reading, writing,
studying or lounging; helping yourself with
perfect freedom to books and writing materials;
for whatever is in the room is entirely at your
service."

Mildred was beginning to thank him, but
he cut her short with, "Never mind that.
Here's better occupation for you," handing her
a package of letters as he spoke.

She took it with a joyful exclamation.
"Letters from home! oh, I have been so hungry for them."

"Yes," he said, enjoying her delight, "but
don't run away," for she had risen to her feet,
evidently with that intention; "perhaps there
may be a bit here and there that you'd like to
read to me. And if they bring tears to your
eyes, I'll not think the worse of you. Besides
I shall be too busy with my own correspondence
to take notice."

So she sat down again and presently forgot his presence in the interest of those written pages which seemed almost to transport her into the very midst of the dear home circle.

It was a family letter, every one, from her father down to Annis, contributing something; the little ones having each dictated a message to "Sister Milly;" but the greater part was from her mother, giving in pleasing detail the doings, sayings and plannings in their little world, the small successes and failures, the apparently trivial occurrences, the little joys and sorrows, little trials and vexations and little pleasures that make or mar the happiness of daily home life.

The mother's sweet, loving, trustful spirit breathed through it all. There were little jests that brought the smile to Mildred's lips or made her laugh outright—and these she read aloud to her uncle:—there were words of faith and patience that filled her eyes with tears; then at the last wise, tender, motherly counsels that stirred her heart to its inmost depths.

She would have given a great deal at that moment to be at home again, within sound of that beloved voice, looking into the dear eyes, feeling the gentle touch of the soft caressing hand. Oh, could she stay away for months?

The tears would come. She rose, crossed the room and stood before a painting, with her back to her uncle, who at that instant seemed wholly absorbed in a business letter which he held in his hand.

Recovering herself, she came back to the table.

Mr. Dinsmore looked up.

"I think we must have a ride to-morrow morning, Milly, you and Adelaide and I, shall it be at nine o'clock?"

Her eyes grew bright and her cheeks flushed with pleasure. She was very fond of riding on horseback.

"I shall be delighted to go, uncle," she said, "and can be ready at any hour that may suit you best."

He considered a moment.

"I should not be surprised if you and Adie find yourselves inclined to take a long morning nap after your journey," he said, "We will say directly after breakfast, which will not be earlier than nine. Now I see you are wanting to retire; so bid me good night and away with you to slumbers sweet," and with a fatherly kiss he dismissed her.

Mildred's room was bright, warm and cheery as she had left it. Rachel was not there; and the trunks had vanished also, but the opening of wardrobe doors and bureau drawers showed their contents neatly bestowed therein.

An easy chair stood invitingly before the fire and dropping into it Mildred gave her letter a second perusal, mingling laughter and tears over it as before.

She sighed softly to herself as she folded it up, then glancing about the spacious, handsomely appointed room, smiled at thought of the contrast between her present circumstances and surroundings and those of a few weeks ago, when she was occupying a small, very plainly furnished room, and instead of having a maid at her beck and call, was constantly waiting upon and working for others.

The rest and ease of the present were certainly very enjoyable, yet she had no desire that the change should become a permanent one; home with all its toils and cares was still the sweetest, dearest place on earth.

Rachel came in to replenish the fire and ask if there was anything more she could do for the young lady's comfort.

"No, thank you, my wants are fully supplied," Mildred said with a smile. "I think I shall get ready for bed now."

"Den missy want her slippers and night

clo's," remarked the girl hastening to bring them. "Shall dis chile' take down yo' hair and brush um out?"

"Yes," Mildred said; "when I have put on my dressing gown; and I'll read to you while you do it."

"Tank you, missy, dis child be berry glad to hear readin'," the girl answered with a look of pleasure, "can't read none herself and neber expects to know how. Dat's for white folks."

"Then I'll read the Bible to you every night and morning while you do up my hair," Mildred said. "It is God's word, Rachel; his letter to tell us the way to heaven and we need to know what it says."

"Spect we does, miss," responded the girl, with wide open, wondering eyes fixed on Mildred's face. "But nobody neber tole me dat befo'."

"Then here is work for me to do for the Master," thought Mildred, and sent up a silent petition, "Lord, teach me how to lead her to thee."

Chapter Sebenth.

'O thou child of many prayers !
Life hath quicksands, life hath snares ! "
—LONGFELLOW.

A BRIGHT ray of sunshine stealing in between
the silken curtains fell athwart Mildred's eyes
and awoke her.

The fire was blazing cheerily on the hearth,
Rachel was at hand to wait upon her, and she
found it by no means unpleasant to sit still and
have her hair skilfully arranged for her instead
of doing the work with her own hands, as she
had been accustomed to do since she was quite
a little girl.

She occupied herself the while in reading
aloud from the Bible, according to promise, and
Rachel seemed well pleased to listen.

Her toilet completed, Mildred went to the
library to answer her letter, while waiting for
the breakfast bell, and there Mr. Dinsmore
found her.

" That is quite right," he said. " Send my

love to them all. But don't close your letter
yet, you'll want to tell your mother about your
~ide. We'll take one that used to be a favorite
with her."

Mildred looked up brightly. " I shall enjoy
it all the more for knowing that."

" You are accustomed to riding on horseback ? " he said inquiringly.

" Enough to be able to keep my seat on a
well behaved steed," she answered laughingly.
" I hope to improve very much under your
tuition, Uncle Dinsmore."

" Gyp, the pony I have assigned to you
while you stay, is quite safe, I think; sufficiently spirited but well trained," he said, giving her his arm to conduct her into the breakfast room, for the bell had rung.

" I hear you are going to ride, Mildred,"
Mrs. Dinsmore remarked as they rose from the
table. " Have you a riding habit ? "

Mildred was very glad to be able to reply
in the affirmative.

The horses were already at the door.

She hurried to her room and was down
again in a few minutes arrayed in a manner
that entirely satisfied Mrs. Dinsmore.

It was a delicious morning, riders and steeds
seemed alike in fine spirits, and Mildred had

seldom found anything more enjoyable than the brisk canter of the next hour over a good road and through new and pleasing scenes.

On their return Mrs. Dinsmore followed her to her room.

"You must have some of your dresses made at once, Mildred," she said. "Can you get out the materials and come now to the sewing-room to be fitted? The black silk should be first, I think, and finished this week, that you may have it to wear to church next Sunday."

"You are very kind, aunt," Mildred said, looking much pleased; "but are not the services of your seamstresses needed just now for yourself and the children?"

"No; there is nothing hurrying," was the reply; "we all had fall dresses made up in Philadelphia, and you must be prepared to show yourself to visitors; for our friends and neighbors will soon be calling on you, as well as on us; of course I shall take pride in having them find my husband's niece suitably attired."

Mildred was nothing loath to accept the offer; in fact was filled with an eager desire, natural to her age, to see how all these beautiful things would look when made up, and how well they would become her.

But her love of independence and the indus-

trious habits in which she had been trained,
alike forbade her to leave all the work to Mrs.
Dinsmore's maids; her own deft and busy
fingers accomplished no small share of it; the
greater part of every day for the next two or
three weeks being occupied in that way.

Mrs. Dinsmore disliked exertion of any kind
and seldom took a needle in her hand, but she
had no distaste toward seeing others employed,
and generally spent her mornings lounging in
the sewing-room, ready to give her opinion in
regard to styles of trimming, and so forth, and
enjoying a comfortable sense of conferring a
great favor thereby.

The black silk was completed in time to be
worn on Mildred's first Sunday at Roselands,
and Mrs. Dinsmore, subjecting her to a careful
scrutiny when she came down ready dressed for
church, assured her that she was quite a stylish
looking young lady, whom she herself was not
ashamed to exhibit to her acquaintance as belonging to the Dinsmore family.

A glance into a pier glass in the drawing-
room told Mildred the compliment was not un-
deserved, and I fear there was no little gratified
vanity in the smile with which she turned away
and followed her aunt to the carriage waiting
for them at the door, and that the consciousness

of her finery and its becomingness seriously interfered with the heartiness of her devotions in the house of God, and the attention she should have given to the preaching of the Word, and services of prayer and praise.

She was in some measure aware of this herself, and felt condemned on account of it; but was not helped to recover lost ground by the worldly conversation carried on about her during the greater part of the day.

There was a good deal of friendly chat in the vestibule of the church, after the close of the services, neighbors and acquaintances gathering about the Dinsmores to welcome and congratulate them on their return from their late trip, and inquire concerning their health and enjoyment of their lengthened sojourn in the North.

Mr. Dinsmore was extremely hospitable and fond of entertaining his friends, nor had he any scruples about doing so on the Sabbath; and at his urgent invitation two gentlemen and a very gayly dressed and lively young lady accompanied his family and himself to Roselands to dine and spend the remainder of the day.

The talk was just what it might have been on any other occasion; of politics, amusements, dress, anything and everything but the topics suited to the sacredness of the day; and Mil dred, while yielding to the temptation to join in it, felt painfully conscious that in so doing she was not obeying the command, " Remember the Sabbath day to keep it holy."

It was late in the evening when the visitors left, and she retired to her room weary and sleepy, hurried through the form of devotion, giving but little heart to it, and was soon in bed and asleep.

She tried to do better the next morning, but her thoughts ran very much on dress and the vanities of earth.

" How could she help that?" she asked herself, half despairingly, half in excuse, "she must assist in making her clothes, and decide, too, how it should be done."

Another dress was begun that day, and head and hands were fully occupied over it.

Her uncle insisted on a ride or walk every day, callers began to come, hours had to be spent in the drawing-room, and work on the new dresses to be pushed all the harder the rest of the day to recover lost time.

Then she must attire herself in her most becoming finery, and drive out with Mrs. Dinsmore to return her calls, during which the talk generally ran upon the merest trifles, furnishing no food for mind or heart.

Flatteries and compliments were showered upon our heroine, for she was pretty, graceful and refined, quick at repartee, self-possessed, without being conceited, well informed for her years, and a good conversationalist.

Her aunt and uncle were altoge.her satisfied with the impression she made; but her parents would have been sorely troubled could they have known how the world and its vanities were engrossing the thoughts of their beloved child, to the exclusion of better things.

There were brilliant entertainments given in her honor; first, by Mrs. Dinsmore, afterward by others who had been her invited guests.

The weather continuing remarkably mild and pleasant for some weeks, there were excursions gotten up to various points of interest in the vicinity; there were dinner parties and tea drinkings; days when the house was filled with gay company from morning to night, or when Mr. and Mrs. Dinsmore visited in like manner at the houses of neighboring planters, taking Mildred with them.

Then there were drives to the city: in the daytime to shop for more finery, in the evening for the purpose of attending some place of amusement,—now a concert, now a lecture, and at length the opera and the theatre.

Into these latter and questionable, not to say forbidden, places of resort, to one reared as Mildred had been, she was at first decoyed ; but becoming intoxicated with their sensual sweets, she went again and again of her own free will.

Thus for a month or more she ran a giddy round of worldly pleasures, scarcely taking time to think, and refusing to listen to the warnings and upbraidings of conscience.

But her gayeties began to tell unfavorably upon her health, the recovery of which had been her principal object in leaving home, and she was obliged to relinquish them in part.

Then a long storm set in, confining her to the house for a week, and keeping away visitors. She was forced to stop and consider, and a long, loving letter from her mother coming just then, freighted with words of Christian counsel, had a blessed effect in helping to open her eyes to her guilt and danger.

In the silence and solitude of her room, the sighing of the wind without, and the rain and sleet beating against the windows, the only sounds that reached her ear, Mildred read and wept over this letter, and over the mental review of the life she had been leading since coming to Roselands.

To a mere worldling it might have seemed innocent enough, but not so to Mildred's enlightened conscience; a butterfly existence was not the end for which she had been created; yet she could not shut her eyes to the fact that that was the best that could be said of her life of late; she had been neither doing nor getting any good, but rather the contrary—injuring her health by her dissipations, setting an example of worldliness, and falling behind in the Christian race.

She had not neglected the forms of religious service,—had attended church every Sunday, read her Bible, and repeated a prayer night and morning; but all, as she now saw with grief and shame, with a sadly wandering heart, thoughts full of dress and earthly vanities.

Alas! how far she had wandered out of the way in which she had covenanted to walk! and that though she had proved in days past, that "Wisdom's ways were ways of pleasantness, and all her paths were peace."

And as she questioned with herself whether she had found real enjoyment in these by-paths of worldliness and sin, she was forced to acknowledge that in spite of much thoughtless gayety and mirth, there had been no genuine.

solid happiness, but instead a secret uneasiness
which she vainly strove to banish, and could
only forget for a time in the giddy round of
amusement.

Should she go on as she had begun? No:
by the help of God she would turn and find
again the path she had left; even as her mother
in this timely letter advised and entreated.

Mrs. Keith knew to some extent, the worldly
atmosphere of the house into which her young
daughter had gone, and she had written with
the fear in her heart that Mildred might suc-
cumb to its temptations even as she had done.

She entreated her to be on her guard, watching unto prayer and thus keeping close to the
Master.

"And, dear daughter," she added, "should
you ever find that you have wandered, lose not
a moment in returning to him and pleading for
cleansing, for pardon, and restoration to his
favor through his own precious blood. Let not
Satan tempt you to stay away one moment with
the lie that the Lord is not ever waiting to be
gracious and ever ready and willing to forgive;
or that he would have you delay till your repentance is deeper or you have done something
to atone in some measure for your sin.

"God's time is always now; to the backslider in heart or life, as well as to the impenitent sinner; and to both he says: 'Him that cometh unto me, I will in no wise cast out!'"

Chapter Eighth.

" I have deeply felt
The mockery of the hollow shrine at which my spirit knelt."
WHITTIER.

MILDRED had been alone for several hours; —very profitable ones to her—when opening the door in answer to a gentle rap, she found Mr. Dinsmore standing there.

"If you will invite me in," he said with a smile, "I may perhaps accept."

"Do come in, uncle," she replied, returning the smile; "it is very pleasant here, and I can give you a warm welcome. See, my fire is blazing cheerily; and does not that easy chair look inviting?"

"Yes," he answered, taking her hand and gazing searchingly into her face, seeing something there that puzzled him greatly; for though the traces of tears were very evident, it wore a look of peace that had been foreign to it of late, "brt what is the matter? not bad news from home, I hope."

"No, oh no!" she said, "they were all wel and nothing amiss when mother wrote," but her eyes filled and her lips quivered as she spoke.

"Homesick, I'm afraid," he said kindly, patting and stroking the hand he held; "the natural effect of news from there, I suppose; especially in this wretched weather; but don't give up to it, my dear. We'll find ways to make the time pass pleasantly spite of the storm; home sports, amusing books."

"You are very kind always, dear uncle," she said with a grateful look, "but it is not that; I have been living too much for mere amusement of late."

And with burning cheeks and tear-dimmed eyes, she went on to explain, in a few rapid sentences, how condemned she felt on account of the waste of time and opportunities for improvement, and the worldly conformity of which she had been guilty; and how she had determined, by God's help, to do so no more.

He listened in much surprise, but did not interrupt her.

When she had finished, there was a moment's silence, she sitting with downcast eyes, her breast still heaving with emotion; he gazing musingly into the fire.

Presently he turned to her again with a kindly smile.

"Thank you, my dear, for your confidence," he said pleasantly, "but really, I do not see that you have done anything to be distressed about. It strikes me you were fairly entitled to a few weeks of play-time, after the fatigues of that long nursing and the journey here."

"Perhaps so," she said, "but I haven't taken just the right sort; so much excitement, and such late hours have wearied instead of resting me physically, and on my spiritual nature the effect has been still worse. I blame no one but myself," she added humbly, and with a deprecating look into his grave, somewhat troubled face.

"I'm afraid I have been your tempter," he said, "though I meant well. But I ought to have remembered the strict ideas entertained by your parents, and in which they had brought you up. Well, what can I do to retrieve my error, and to help you in living as you think you should?"

"It mostly depends upon myself, I think," she answered thoughtfully, "but if you will not oppose me in declining invitations to what I deem to be wrong or questionable amuse-

ments, and will excuse me from attendance in
the drawing-room on Sundays, when there is
company it will help me very much."

"My dear girl," he returned, "you are of
course perfectly free to do exactly as you
please in both respects. We appreciate your
society, but if you think best to withdraw it
from us, we can only submit. I will arrange
with Mrs. Dinsmore that young people shall be
invited on week days and only older people,
whom you will not feel called upon to entertain, on Sundays."

She thanked him warmly.

"And you will give up the opera and theatre?" he said inquiringly, "I thought you enjoyed them very much."

"I did," she answered, blushing.

"Then why resign so innocent a pleasure?"

"It is not innocent for me, uncle," she said,
lifting her glistening eyes to his, "it utterly
destroys the spirit of devotion. I come from
them with my mind full of the play, and
thoughts about dress and the gay people I
have seen, and with no heart for prayer or the
study of God's word. And the short-lived
pleasure I derive from them is nothing to be
compared with the sweet peace and joy they
rob me of."

" But if you persist in such a course cf conduct, you will be sneered at as self-righteous, puritanical, and what not; politely to your face, more disagreeably behind your back."

"I am willing to be singular for Christ," she answered, her eyes kindling, "Oh, how little that would be to bear for him compared with what he endured for me! how much less I resign than multitudes of others have given up for him! Moses chose 'rather to suffer affliction with the people of God, than to enjoy the pleasures of sin for a season, esteeming the reproach of Christ greater riches than the treasures in Egypt.'"

" And you purpose to begin doing something in the way of study and the cultivation of your accomplishments?" he said inquiringly, not unwilling to change the subject of conversation.

" Yes, uncle, I should like to accept your generous offer to let me share the instructions of Adelaide's masters in music and painting, French and German; and Miss Worth's in the higher mathematics."

" All that will keep you pretty busy even without the reading you are sure to do," he commented with a smile.

" Usefully employed," she answered bright-

ly "and that, I have learned from experience
is the way to be happy."

The first sneer Mildred had to bear came
from Mrs. Dinsmore, who heard with great
vexation her husband's report of the young
girl's resolve.

"Ridiculous!" she exclaimed. "If there's
anything I do detest and despise, it is your
rigid, puritanical sectary, who stands ready to
cry out 'sinful! wicked!' at every sort of enjoyment! I am too much provoked. She is
really a pretty and lady-like girl, and has
attracted a good deal of attention; so that I was
actually growing quite proud of her, and took
pleasure in showing her off.

"But that is all over now, of course, and
there'll be no end to the annoyance I shall have
to endure in hearing her criticized for her odd behavior, and in parrying questions and remarks
as to how she came by such strange notions."

"Well, my dear, it can't be helped," Mr.
Dinsmore responded, between a smile and a
sigh, "but if I were you I should very decidedly snub any one who should offer a disparag-
ing remark about her to me. Being myself,
I certainly intend to do so."

"Can't be helped! I believe you could
reason her out of it if you would!"

"I am flattered by your belief, but do not share it," he said with a bow of acknowledgment; "nor if I did, would I attempt to change her views. 'Twould be too great a responsibility and a breach of the trust her parents have reposed in me."

The conversation was here brought to a conclusion by the summons to the dinner table.

Mildred made her appearance with the rest and was greeted by Mrs. Dinsmore with a cold inquiry after her health, followed by a covert taunt in regard to her resolve to forsake the worldly amusements in which she had of late indulged.

Mildred bore it with patience and humility, "not answering again," though the flushing of her cheek showed that she felt the unkindness keenly enough.

"Do you intend to make a complete hermit of yourself and go nowhere at all?" queried the irate lady.

"Oh, no, aunt," returned Mildred pleasantly, "I hope still to take walks, rides and drives; and do not object to calls and social visits, or to concerts or lectures; unless attending necessitates the keeping of later hours than are good for my health."

"Humph! 'twould have been wiser to my

thinking, if you had begun as you meant to continue."

" Yes, aunt, it would," Mildred said, again coloring deeply, "and I wish I had; but it i better to do right at last than not at all. Do you not think so ?"

" Don't ask me," sharply. "Adelaide, Louise and Lora, you may consider yourselves fortunate in having a cousin who is more capable of deciding questions of duty than your parents, I trust you will not fail to profit by her excellent example ; not that which she has set, you will observe, but that which she is going to set you in the future."

The children giggled, while Mildred colored more deeply than before.

A frown had gathered on Mr. Dinsmore's brow.

" Children, if you cannot behave properly you must leave the table," he said sternly ; then with a displeased look at his wife, "I for one highly approve of Mildred's resolve to do what she considers her duty; and it is my desire that she be allowed to follow the dictates of her conscience in peace."

Mr Dinsmore was an indulgent husband and seldom found fault with anything his wife chose to do or say but experience had taught her that when he did interfere, she might as well submit at once. The subject was dropped and never revived again in his presence.

With her accustomed promptness and energy Mildred sought out Miss Worth that very afternoon, made arrangements for recitations, and began her studies.

She determined to devote four hours a day to them and her accomplishments. As she was accustomed to early rising and the breakfast hour at Roselands was late, it would not be difficult, she thought, to secure two hours before that meal ; the other two she would take during Mrs. Dinsmore's afternoon siesta and the elaborate toilet which usually followed ; and thus be as much as ever at that lady's command as a companion either at home or abroad.

Mrs. Dinsmore had few resources within herself, was a martyr to ennui and could not bear to be alone ; and Mildred esteemed it both a duty and a pleasure to do all in her power to add to the comfort and enjoyment of her kind entertainers ; she had succeeded thus far in doing so, in some measure, to all, from her uncle down to Baby Enna.

The children had found out weeks ago that Cousin Milly possessed an apparently inexhaustible fund of nursery tales and songs, and could teach them many amusing games.

They would have been glad to monopolize her, and entered many a complaint of the shortness and infrequency of her visits to the nursery.

Thinking of that now, she resolved to try to give them more of her time and attention; perhaps she could mingle some instruction with the amusement she furnished them; and she would be very glad to do so; for her heart was filled with pity for the young things as she thought of the great difference between their mother and hers; the one absorbed in her own selfish pleasures, and paying no attention to the cultivation of the minds and hearts of her children; the other giving herself with earnest, whole-souled devotion to seeking the best interests of her darlings, teaching and training them for happiness and usefulness here and hereafter.

"Precious mother! what a blessing to have been born your child," Mildred mentally exclaimed as she thus dwelt upon the contrast between the two, recalling with tear-dimmed eyes the loving care that had surrounded her from her very birth and in which each brother and sister had an equal share.

While Mildred thus laid her plans, Mrs. Dinsmore was somewhat similarly employed. Reclining upon a softly cushioned couch in her boudoir, idly listening to the pattering of the rain against the window, she mused in discontented mood of Mildred, and her unexpected resolve. It interfered with her schemes, for she had purposed filling the house with gay young company during the approaching Christmas holidays and making the two weeks one continued round of festivity.

To be sure she could do so still, but Mildred's refusal to take part in much of the sport would throw a damper upon the enjoyment of the others; besides giving occasion for unpleasant criticisms.

Mrs. Dinsmore's vexations increased as she turned the matter over in her mind.

But a bright thought struck her, and starting up with something like energy, she exclaimed, half aloud; "Why that's the very thing! and I'll do it at once. Hagar," addressing her maid, "bring me my writing desk."

Chapter Ninth.

" There's not a joy the world can give like that it takes away."
BYRON.

"DEAR me! another dull, rainy, tedious day!" sighed Mrs. Dinsmore the next morning, as she turned from the breakfast-table, walked to the window and looked out upon the gardens and fields where everything was dripping with wet, "will the storm never end? No hope of visitors to-day, or of setting out to see anybody. I shall be literally eaten up with ennui."

"Here's Mildred," remarked Mr. Dinsmore, "I have always found her good company."

"Humph! she has no time to waste upon me."

"I am quite at your service, Aunt," said our heroine pleasantly.

"Indeed! what's to become of your all-important studies?"

"They have already had two hours devoted to them this morning, besides two last night; so I think I have fairly earned the pleasure of your society for so much of the day as you care to have mine," returned the girl, in a sprightly tone.

Mrs. Dinsmore looked languidly surprised and pleased.

" You are an odd girl to rise so early when you might just as well indulge in a morning nap," she said.

" I don't find it difficult if I have gotten to bed in good season the night before," said Mildred gayly, "I have been trained to it from childhood ; my father being a firm believer in the old adage,

" Early to bed and early to rise,
Makes a man healthy, wealthy and wise,"

and it is really very pleasant after one is fairly up and dressed."

" Yes ; and I dare say we would all be the oetter for it if we would follow your example," said Mr. Dinsmore.

" You are altogether mistaken as far as I am concerned," remarked his wife pettishly, " my best sleep is in the morning."

" I suppose people differ about that as well as in the amount of sleep they require," observed Mildred, " some needing eight hours, while others can do quite as well with only four.

"Yes,' admitted her uncle, "constitutions differ, and I have no idea of asking my wife to give up her morning nap. There is a possibility of carrying the thing to an extreme. Remember that, Miss Milly," he added, playfully, "and don't let that sensitive conscience of yours force you up at unchristian hours."

"And how am I to decide what are such, sir?" she asked, laughing.

Mildred laid herself out that day for her aunt's entertainment, and with a success that restored her almost entirely to favor; at least, for the time being.

The following day there was a slight abatement in the storm, and some gentlemen called.

One, a young man who had been her escort on several occasions, and whom Mildred liked very much as a friend, inquired particularly for her.

He had come with an invitation to a public ball to be given a week later by a military club of which he was a member, and to ask that he might be her escort thither.

Mildred declined with thanks.

He seemed much disappointed, and pressed for her reasons.

"I have several, Mr. Landreth," she said, coloring slightly, but meeting his eye unflinchingly; I find that late hours injure my health ; that is one ; another is that I have been brought up to consider it wrong to attend balls."

" Why more so than going to the theatre?" he asked.

" I do not know that it is."

" Excuse me, but you go there."

" It is true ; I have been several times, but that was very wrong in me, and I do not intend to go again," Mildred said, humbly, yet firmly, though the color deepened on her cheek and her voice trembled slightly.

The words had cost her no small effort, but she was glad when they were spoken ; it seemed to lift a load from her heart and conscience.

Mr. Landreth looked full of regret and surprise.

" I am sorry," he said, " will it be taking too great a liberty to ask why you think it wrong ?"

It seemed a difficult and trying thing to undertake. Mildred hesitated a moment, her eyes cast down, her cheeks burning; but remembering the words of the Master, " Whosoever, therefore, shall confess me before men, him will I confess also before my father which is in heaven. But whosoever shall deny me before men, him will I also deny before my father which is in heaven," she answered.

" Because I profess to be a follower of the Lord Jesus Christ, and as such, to take his word as my rule of faith and practice. That word bids us ' whether, therefore, ye eat or drink, or whatsoever ye do, do all to the glory of God,' and I find it impossible to obey that command in attending such places of worldly amusement.'

" You are very young to give up all pleasure," he said, with an involuntary sigh, " one ought to have some happiness, some enjoyment in youth. I should say it would be quite time enough to resign all these things when we arrive at middle age."

"Ah, you quite mistake me, Mr. Landreth," she answered, looking up brightly, "I only resign a few miserable unsatisfying pleasures for those that are infinitely higher and more enduring."

He gazed at her incredulously.

" Religion has always seemed to me a very gloomy thing," he said, " very good and valuable on a deathbed, no doubt, but---I should ather do without it till then, I must confess."

" I would not," she answered earnestly, ' I

want it to sweeten my life all the way through. Mr. Landreth, believe me, it does do that as nothing else can. I have found it so in my own limited experience, and I know that my parents have in theirs, which has extended over so many more years."

" I have seen them wonderfully sustained by it under sore trials, and have noticed that in times of happiness and prosperity it more than doubled their joy and gladness. ' Godliness with contentment is great gain ! ' "

"Well, Miss Keith," he said, after a moment's pause, " I think you deserve that it should be gain to you in some way, since you sacrifice so much for its sake."

" Ah, you are determined to consider it a sacrifice, I see," she returned smiling. " And I deserve that you should," she added sorrow· fully.

" Excuse me," he said, " I do not doubt your sincerity, but the Christians with whom I am most intimately acquainted, seem to me anything but happy ; if I may judge from their countenances and the gloomy austerity of their lives."

"Ah, if I could only show you my mother ! ' exclaimed Mildred, " if you could know her as I do, you would tell a different story."

" Mildred afterward repeated this last remark of Mr. Landreth's to her aunt.

" Yes," said Mrs. Dinsmore with an expres-
sive shrug of the shoulders, " I know all about
that, and you will understand it too, when you
have seen his aunt—or rather his uncle's wife—
Mrs. James Landreth, and her house. By the
way, we must call there ; she called on me one
day not long since, when we were out."

" What is she like ? " asked Mildred.

" Don't ask ; wait till you see her ; no description could do her justice. At least none
that I could give," Mrs. Dinsmore answered, a
little impatiently.

Mildred's curiosity was excited and she was
eager to make the proposed call.

After a few days' delay for good roads and
good weather, she and her aunt set out, taking
an early start, as they had a drive of some miles
before them, and designed paying several other
visits.

" The Landreths live in the suburbs of the
city," Mrs. Dinsmore remarked, " and I have
ordered Ajax to drive there first. I always like
to get disagreeable things over."

" I wish," said Mildred, " that one might
confine one's calls to those whom it is a real
pleasure to visit. '

"Of course it would be very delightful if one could," said her aunt, "but there is no use in talking about it; you can't tell people, I don't wish to keep up acquaintance with you because your society is not agreeable to me."

"No, of course not," returned Mildred laughing. "Do you suppose Mrs. Landreth calls on us, too, because the customs of society require it?"

"Really I can't tell. I know she doesn't enjoy it; because I am not one of her sort. I'm certain she looks upon me as a very worldly minded, wicked woman, a kind of heathen in fact, and perhaps she considers herself doing missionary work in coming to see me."

"The house and grounds are handsome," Mildred remarked with some surprise, as they alighted at Mr. Landreth's door.

"Outside," Mrs. Dinsmore returned significantly.

Mrs. Landreth was at home and they were shown into the drawing-room.

It was a spacious, rather dreary looking apartment, very plainly furnished and almost wholly destitute of ornament, with the exception of a few old family portraits. The only really attractive objects in the room were a brightly blazing fire and a very fine painting over the mantel.

This last riveted Mildred's attention in a moment, and she exclaimed at its beauty.

"Yes," whispered Mrs. Dinsmore, "it's the one handsome thing in the house, and she s always at her husband to sell it."

"Why?" and Mildred's look expressed unfeigned astonishment.

"Praise it to her and you will hear all about it."

Their hostess entered. She was tall, angular, of sallow complexion, and strong featured. Her black hair, streaked here and there with grey, was drawn straight back from a forehead crossed by many lines.

Caps were much worn even by youthful matrons at that day, but Mrs. Landreth had resorted to no such artifice to conceal from view the partially bald spot on the top of her head; neither did the close fitting, black stuff gown hide one angle of her stiff, ungainly figure.

Her movements were ungraceful, her countenance was solemn as might have befitted a funeral occasion

"She is certainly far from pleasing in appearance," thought Mildred, furtively scanning the unattractive face, and mentally contrasting it with the dear, bright, cheerful one that had made the sunshine of her childhood's home.

Mrs. Landreth's face served as a good foil even to Mrs. Dinsmore's faded beauty; a fact of which that lady was by no means unaware or intolerant.

The two conversed together for some minutes; Mildred sitting silently by. They were speaking of the weather, then of some common acquaintance of whom she knew nothing, and not feeling interested she half unconsciously suffered her eyes to wander about the room.

"You do not find much to admire here?" Mrs. Landreth said, interrogatively, turning abruptly to her. "There are no pretty trifles scattered here and there as at Roselands."

"I admire that painting over the mantel exceedingly," Mildred answered with a blush, and turning her gaze upon it again; "such a lovely, sunny landscape! it gives one a restful feeling just to look at it."

"Yes, it is a fine painting, but I have often told my husband that I think he committed a sin in putting so much money into an unnecessary luxury; something we could do perfectly well without. The Bible bids us be content with food and raiment; and we ought not to indulge ourselves in anything more; or to

spend much on them while there are so many
deserving objects of charity in the world.   That
is why you find me so plain in my attire and in
the furnishing of my house.

"Mr. Landreth holds different views and
would like house and wife to look as well as
those of his neighbors, as he often says ; but I
must act according to the dictates of my conscience."

"But don't you think it a duty to try to
please your husband and make his home attractive ? " Mildred asked modestly.   " I know
my mother considers it hers and her great
pleasure also."

"Quite natural then that you should ; but
doubtless I am an older woman than she ; and
years should teach wisdom," rejoined Mrs.
Landreth, somewhat loftily.

"Yes, madam, I suppose they should ; but
do you think people are always wise just in proportion to their age ? "

"Of course not always.   Mr. Landreth is
older than I.

"But now to return to the original topic
We are taught that we ought to practice self-
denial and to give liberally to the poor.   The
interest of the money paid for that picture
(five thousand dollars) would enable me to

largely increase, my benefactions, if I had it.
And besides how much useful work the artist
might have done in the time he spent—wasted
one may well say—in painting it."

" I cannot think the time was wasted, or that
God would have given him the talent if he were
not to use it, or that it is wrong to surround ourselves with beautiful things if we have the
means," ventured Mildred, still thinking of her
mother's practice and the opinions she had
heard her express.

Mrs. Landreth gave her a look that said
as plainly as words, " I consider you a very
opinionated and silly young person," and Mrs.
Dinsmore arose to take leave.

" That woman," she remarked as she threw
herself back in her carriage, " has done more
to disgust me with religion than anybody or
anything else ! She is always parading her self-
denial and benevolence, always looks as solemn
as if it was a sin to laugh, seems unhappy herself and anxious to make everybody else so.
If that is Christianity I want none of it ! and I
know that is just how Charlie Landreth feels !"

" But it isn't Christianity, aunt," Mildred
said earnestly. " And do you not know some
Christians who are very different ? "

" Yes there's Mrs. Travilla, at Ion, where

we are going now. She is always cheerful, quite merry at times, and a great deal better woman, to my thinking, than Mrs. Landreth, though she doesn't appear to think so herself. In fact she's too good for me; gives me an uncomfortable sense of my own inferiority in that respect."

" Are the Landreths poor ? " asked Mildred.

"Poor ; child," exclaimed Mrs. Dinsmore, laughing. " Wouldn't Charlie and his uncle be mortified if they could hear that question ! Poor! no, indeed ! Mr. Landreth could afford twenty paintings as costly as that; but he isn't allowed to enjoy one, and the house looks forlorn and comfortless from garret to cellar."

" And is she really so benevolent ? "

" She gives a great deal to missions, and to the poor, and the church, but I think it would be well for her to remember that charity begins at home, and to bestow a little kindness upon her husband and his nephew. If they were beggars she would perhaps think it worth while to pay some attention to their comfort; as it is they get nothing from her but sermons and lectures on their worldliness and wickedness."

" But Mr. Charlie Landreth doesn't seem to me like a bad young man," said Mildred, in surprise.

" He isn't," said Mrs. Dinsmore, " he's a thorough gentleman and has no vices; there isn't a finer young man the country round. But he isn't pious; so of course she considers him a reprobate."

" I have heard my mother speak of Mrs. Travilla as a lovely Christian lady and an intimate friend of Aunt Eva," said Mildred, willing to introduce a new topic.

" Yes ; and I always feel that she is making comparisons, unfavorable to me of course, between Mr. Dinsmore's first wife and myself. So I can hardly be expected to be very fond of her."

" But isn't it possible that you may be mistaken, Aunt Isabel ? "

" I'm not given to fancies," was the ungracious rejoinder.

Then there was a short silence broken presently by a query from Mildred.

" Has Mrs. Travilla any daughters ? "

" No ; only a son; and he's away in Europe. The families—ours and theirs—have always been intimate, Edward Travilla and Horace inseparable companions, and they went to Europe together."

" It seems odd I should have been here so long without meeting Mrs. Travilla."

"She has been away; went North with her son, and did not return till quite recently. She called at Roselands the same day Mrs. Landreth did and inquired for you."

Mildred was greatly pleased with both Ion and its mistress.

The grounds were extensive, beautiful and well cared for, the house, a fine old mansion handsomely furnished, abounded in tasteful ornamentation; there were articles of *vertu* scattered through its rooms—rare and costly bits of painting and sculpture. Also less expensive adornments, singing birds and blooming plants and flowers; all showing a refined and cultivated taste, and forming together a most harmonious and charming whole.

Mrs. Travilla was perhaps some years older than Mrs. Dinsmore, and with her, too, youthful bloom had fled; but it had given place to beauty of another and higher order—the illumination of a richly cultivated mind and heart.

She was attired with simple elegance and a due regard to her age, circumstances and what best became her style of beauty. Her manner was simple and cordial, her conversation sprightly, her voice low and sweet toned.

"You resemble your mother," she said with a kindly smile, taking Mildred's hand in parting, and gazing earnestly into her face. " I re member her well for I saw a good deal of her in her visits to Roselands: and truly to know her was to love her. Some day soon, if your aunt can spare you, you must spend a day with me, and we will have a long talk about her. I want to hear all you have to tell."

"Oh, I should be delighted!" Mildred exclaimed, her cheeks glowing, her eyes sparkling. Mrs. Travilla had found the way to her heart, and from that moment they were fast friends.

Chapter Tenth.

" There is a Friend that sticketh closer than a brother."
PROVERBS 18 : 24.

You found Mrs. Travilla a decided contrast to the other lady," remarked Mrs. Dinsmore, as they drove down the avenue at Ion; "pray, which do you think is right in her religious views?"

"There is no question in my mind as to which is the more attractive," said Mildred, "or which seems to recommend her religion the most by her looks and ways; yet Mrs. Landreth's self-denial certainly appears commendable, but—oh, I confess that I am really puzzled and must take time to consider."

"Well, I hope you won't pattern after Mrs. Landreth."

"No, never!" Mildred exclaimed, with energy. "I know it cannot be right to make home uninviting and cheerless; my mother has taught me better than that, both by precept and example."

"There is a letter for you, my dear," Mr. Dinsmore said, handing his wife and niece from the carriage.

"From whom?" she asked, with interest

"I have not opened it, but the address is in your sister Delia's hand."

"Ah! then it is just the one I want."

At the tea table Mrs. Dinsmore made an announcement.

"My nieces, Juliet and Reba Marsden, are coming on a visit here. We may expect them to-night or to-morrow."

"To-night?" said Mr. Dinsmore inquiringly. "They come by the stage, eh?"

"Yes; it passes at what hour?"

"Eight; Pomp," to the servant in waiting. "tell Aunt Phœbe to have a hot supper ready at quarter past eight."

"Young ladies, Aunt?" asked Mildred, looking up with a bright, pleased face.

"Yes, eighteen and twenty. Company for you, I hope."

Mildred slipped away to her own room shortly before the time for the arrival of the stage. She had a lesson to prepare, a letter to write, and thought her aunt would want to have her nieces to herself for the first hour or two. Besides Mrs. Dinsmore had expressed an intention to send them to bed betimes, that they might be fresh for the ball which was to come off the next evening.

On the stairway Mildred met her three cousins, Adelaide, Louise, and Lora.

"Study hour's just over, and we're going to the drawing-room," they announced. "We've got leave to stay up and see our cousins when they come."

"That's nice," she answered, "I hope to see them in the morning."

In the hall above, she passed Miss Worth on her way from the schoolroom to her own apartment. She was struck with the weary and sad expression of her face, and paused for an instant, nalf inclined to offer her sympathy, and ask if in anything she could be of service.

But with a slight nod of recognition, the governess glided by, and the next moment Mildred heard her door close, and the key turn in the lock.

"Poor thing! I dare say she is homesick!" thought Mildred, passing on into her own room, which she found, as usual, very bright and cheery; a good fire, a table with an astral lamp, books and writing materials, drawn up near it, an easy chair on the farther side; the one inviting to work, the other to repose.

She had complete.y won Rachel's heart, and the young handmaiden took especial pride and pleasure in arranging everything to " Miss Milly's" liking, and being always ready to wait upon her.

Mildred sat down at the table and opened her books.

" Two hours for these and my letter to mother; then to bed and to sleep, that I may be able to rise early and secure the two morning hours for study before seeing those girls at breakfast," was the thought in her mind.

She set herself to her work with determined energy, but in vain; she could not fix her attention. She conned the words again and again but without taking in their meaning. Miss Worth's sad face kept coming between her and the printed page.

" She is very lonely, she needs a friend, a comforter," whispered the inward voice.

" But she might consider me an intruder, trying to pry into her private affairs, forcing a friendship upon her which she has never sought—and she so much older than I," was the answering thought. " And she is only a governess. Aunt Belle evidently considers her quite beneath her friendship, and might be dis pleased if I put her on an equality with myself."

But Mildred blushed to find herself influenced by such a motive. She too might be a governess some day and she would be none the less a lady; it was an honorable and useful calling; and it ought to be considered far more creditable to earn one's bread thus than to be willing to live upon the labor of others.

"No," she exclaimed half aloud, closing her book and pushing it from her, "that shall not hinder me! but ought I to go?"

Dropping her face into her hands, she sent up a silent petition. "Lord, show me! I desire to acknowledge thee in all my ways, and I know thou wilt fulfill thy gracious promise to direct my paths."

Then she tried to put herself in Miss Worth's place. How utterly lonely the poor governess was among them all! among, and yet not of them. Mrs. Dinsmore would as soon have thought of sympathizing with an automaton as with any of the human creatures employed in her service. Her domestics were comfortably fed and clothed; Miss Worth's liberal salary was always punctually paid; and what more could any of them ask?

As Mildred mentally reviewed the events of the past weeks she realized as never before how entirely apart from them all this one member of the family circle had been—her presence ignored in their familiar chat—except when it related in some way to her duties—her wishes, taste, convenience never consulted, no interest taken in her welfare, no inquiries regarding her health or happiness or as to whether her letters —usually handed to her at the breakfast-table when the others received theirs—brought good news or ill.

Ah, now it came to Mildred's recollection that that morning's mail brought a letter for Miss Worth; and had she not looked a little paler than her wont at dinner? and were there not traces of tears about her eyes?

Her hesitation was at an end. She was quite sure that if bad news had come to her she would be glad to have the sympathy of even a child, or a dumb animal; and only waiting to ask for wisdom to do and say the right thing, she rose and went out into the hall.

The stage had just driven up to the door, and the sounds coming from below told of the arrival of the expected guests, gay, girlish voices mingling with those of her aunt, uncle and cousins.

She lingered a moment thinking how pleasant it would be should those girls prove con-

genial companions to her, then going to Miss
Worth's door she tapped lightly on it.

A step came slowly across the room and the
door opened.

"Excuse me," Mildred said, blushing and
hesitating, "I do not wish to intrude, but I
hought you looked sad and had perhaps heard
ill news; might be homesick, in need of a friend
even if it were one who had only sympathy to
offer."

"Come in, won't you?"

"It is very, very kind, Miss Keith; I did
not expect it; and—and I do want a friend,"
was answered in hurried, tremulous tones, as
Miss Worth stepped back to allow her visitor
to pass in, then closed the door and set a chair
for her near the fire.

A writing desk stood open on the table, an
unfinished letter lying upon it.

"I'm afraid I have disturbed you," Mildred
said, glancing at them. "You are busy?"

"No, I found I could not say what I wished,
or perhaps did not know what I wanted to say,"
the governess answered with a dreary sigh.

Silence fell between them for some moments,
Miss Worth, who had resumed her seat, gazing
abstractedly into the fire, while Mildred was
trying to think what to say, and silently asking

to be directed. But she was not the first to speak "Does life ever seem to you a weary road to travel, Miss Keith? A burden that you would be glad to lay down forever?" asked the governess. "But I forget. You are so young, so happy, that you can know nothing of such an experience. At your age I was gay and light-hearted too; as well I might be—at home in my father's house and abundantly supplied with comforts and luxuries without thought or care of mine. Ah, times are sadly changed with me and all who are nearest and dearest to me. But excuse me! I have no right to obtrude my private griefs upon you."

"Please don't feel so," Mildred said, sympathetic tears springing to her eyes. "I cannot tell you how sorry I am for you! how I would like to comfort you! and I know it is sometimes a relief and comfort just to pour out our sorrows to a fellow creature. And O, Miss Worth, I wish you knew what a comfort it is to tell them all to Jesus!" she added low and feelingly.

"Is it? Do you think he can hear? that he listens? that ho cares?"

The look that accompanied the questions was half eager, half skeptical, and full of unexpressed longing.

"I have not the least doubt of it," Mildred answered with earnest conviction in her tones. "'God over all blessed forever,' he is everywhere present. He has, as he himself declared, all power given unto him in heaven and in earth; and he is so full of love and compassion that he deems nothing that concerns his children, one way or another, too small for his attention. He would not have even the little children turned away when the parents brought them to him, and he cares for the sparrows.

"'Are not two sparrows sold for a farthing? and one of them shall not fall to the ground without your Father. But the very hairs of your head are all numbered. Fear ye not, therefore, ye are of more value than many sparrows.'"

"But I am not one of his children;" sighed the governess. "I have paid no attention to these things, Miss Mildred; I did not seek him in my days of prosperity, and I cannot expect him to care for me now in my adversity."

"But he is so loving and compassionate, so ready to forgive. He proclaims himself 'the Lord, the Lord God, merciful and gracious, long-suffering and abundant in goodness and truth, keeping mercy for thousands, forgiving iniquity and transgression and sin.'

" 'Come now and let us reason together, saith the Lord : though your sins be as scarlet, they shall be as white as snow ; though they be red like crimson they shall be as wool.' Jesus said, ' Him that cometh to me I will in nowise cast out.' You say you want a friend, Miss Worth, and there is none other that can compare with Jesus in love and tenderness, in power and willingness to do all you need."

" A friend," repeated Miss Worth absently, more as if thinking aloud than talking to her visitor, "yes, that is what I need; what I have been longing for for days and weeks; more especially to-night; but," and she turned her face abruptly toward Mildred, while her voice took a touchingly pathetic tone, "I know not how or where to find the One you speak of; nor can I believe that he would receive me if I did ; that he would care to help and comfort me. Why should he ? "

" I don't know, except that he is so good, so kind, so loving!" Mildred said, her eyes shining. " But dare you doubt his word ? the word of him who tells us that he himself is the truth ? "

" Does he say that ? "

" Yes, 'I am the way and the truth and the life.' Oh, believe his love—the love of Christ which passeth knowledge! ' Herein is love,

not that we loved God, but that he loved us
and sent his son to be the propitiation for our
sins.' "

"Ah, but am I included in that word
'our'?"

" 'Come unto me all ye that labor and are
heavy laden and I will give you rest.' 'Whosoever will, let him take the water of life freely.'
Could invitations be more comprehensive?"

"No; I think not. But how, Miss Mildred, how shall I come? I was not religiously
brought up and am very ignorant on these subjects."

" 'With the heart man believeth unto righteousness.' 'Believe on the Lord Jesus Christ
and thou shalt be saved.' "

"But what am I to do?"

" 'Let the wicked forsake his way, and the
unrighteous man his thoughts: and let him return unto the Lord, and he will have mercy
upon him;' quoted Mildred, 'and to our God
for he will abundantly pardon,' 'only believe;'
for by grace are ye saved, through faith; and
that not of yourselves; it is the gift of God.
Not of works, lest any man should boast.'

"Do you not see that Christ has done it all
kept the law for us, borne its penalty in our
stead, and now offers us the justification of our

persons, the sanctification of our natures, and adoption into God's family all as a free gift, the purchase of his blood. We cannot merit it, we cannot buy it; it is 'without money and without price.' All we can do is to accept the offered salvation and forsaking every other hope and trust, lean wholly upon Jesus."

Miss Worth seemed lost in sad perplexing thought, while Mildred's heart went up in silent petition on her behalf.

"Tell it me again," she said at length with emotion ; and Mildred tried to make a clearer statement than before.

" It is so simple and beautiful—God's plan of salvation—" Mildred said in conclusion, " only to give ourselves unreservedly to the Lord and trust wholly in him. Jesus said, ' This is the work of God, that ye believe on him whom he hath sent.' And of his sheep, he says, ' I give unto them eternal life ; and they shall never perish, neither shall any pluck them out of my hand.' "

" Yes ; but I want a friend now :—for this life : its cares, troubles, trials, perplexities. Does he promise that ? " asked the governess, with a wistful, longing look.

" Oh, yes, yes indeed ! in very many places," Mildred said. ' This poor man cried and the

Lord heard him and saved him out of all his troubles.' "

" ' He shall deliver thee in six troubles; yea in seven there shal no evil touch thee.'

" ' Call upon me in the day of trouble: I will deliver thee, and thou shalt glorify me.'

" ' Cast thy burden upon the Lord and he shall sustain thee.'

" ' Be careful for nothing; but in every thing by prayer and supplication with thanksgiving, let your requests be made known unto God. And the peace of God which passeth all understanding, shall keep your hearts and minds through Christ Jesus.' "

Again a few moments of profound silence, while Miss Worth seemed to be thinking deeply, then turning to Mildred, " I cannot express my sense of your kindness," she said, " and—" she paused, hesitated, but went on hurriedly, and with emotion, " I will seek this Friend of whom you have been speaking, for I screly need such an one. But you," she continued with increasing emotion, " you have so generously offered your sympathy, yet refrained, with true delicacy, from showing the least curiosity in regard to my troubles. But it would be a relief to confide in you to some extent, if—if you would care to listen."

"I should be much interested and very glad to be of service," Mildred answered gently. "And I think I need not assure you that your confidence will be sacred."

"No; I am quite certain of that," returned Miss Worth; then went on to give a slight sketch of her past life; or rather of some parts of it; for she did not deem it necessary, or wise, to tell of all the trials which had fallen to her lot.

Her father, she said, had been in the early part of his career a very successful business man, and in her childhood and youth she was surrounded with luxury; but reverses came, loss followed loss, till they were reduced to absolute poverty. Then her father died and the burden of her mother's support, as well as her own and that of a younger sister, fell upon her.

There was an older sister who had been married for some years; but her husband was dissipated and worthless, and she had several little children to provide for as best she could. The mother and Delia, the young sister, lived with her, but Miss Worth paid their board, and clothed them.

The letter received to-day was from Mrs. Marks, the married one, and drew a sad picture of toil, privation, and bitter disappointment.

Her children were sick, her husband came home drunk every night, to threaten and abuse her, and then the mother fretted continually over their reverses and her own ailments, fancied or real; and Delia was dissatisfied because she could not dress like other girls in the school she attended. The letter wound up with a request for a loan, and a hint that the sum paid for board of the mother and sister was too small. Also a little note was inclosed from Delia, asking, indeed almost demanding, money for the purchase of a new dress.

But of these Miss Worth said nothing.

Mildred was full of genuine sympathy, and showed it in a way that was very soothing and comforting.

Yet, after she was gone, the burden rolled back upon the heart of the poor, lonely governess. She sat long over the fire, hands clasped in her lap, head bowed upon her breast, vainly striving to solve the perplexing problem how she was to meet all the demands upon her slender purse.

Her disposition was noble and self sa_rificing; she would have willingly denied herself all superfluities in dress that her mother might not miss her accustomed luxuries, Delia go without finery, or Mrs. Marks and her children

be overworked or underfed; but it would not
do; Mrs. Dinsmore's governess must be many
removes from shabby in her attire.

Chapter Eleventh.

" Self is the medium least refined of all,
    Through which Opinion's searching beam can fall ;
    And passing there, the clearest, steadiest ray,
    Will tinge its light, and turn its line astray."

MOORE.

IT was at the breakfast table the next morning that Mildred had her first sight of the new comers.

They were late in making their appearance, excusing themselves on the ground of fatigue from the journey of the previous day.

Juliet, the elder of the two, was an extremely sentimental young lady ; tall and thin, with fair complexion, pale auburn hair, and faded blue eyes.

The other, Reba, a noisy, rattling, romping, pert young Miss, with staring black eyes, black hair, straight and coarse, and a muddy skin, which she strove with very limited success to conceal with toilet powder and rouge.

She prided herself on being a fast girl, a

good shot with a pistol, and not afraid to mount the wildest horse that could be found.

Her talk was of horses and dogs, race courses and shooting matches; her sister's of beaux, parties and dress.

Juliet had a great deal to say about her summer at Saratoga, and the gentlemen she had met there, especially a certain titled foreigner, whom she spoke of as " that charming, fascinating Count De Lisle."

It came out in the course of the morning, that she had heard from him since her return home in the fall, and would not be surprised if he should follow her to Roselands.

"Pa won't like it if he does," remarked Reba. " He thinks he's a fortune-hunter, with nothing to recommend him but his title, and that very likely it is all a pretence. And I am inclined to think pa is right, and that the fellow is not even a foreigner."

" As if your opinion was of the least consequence!" sneered her sister. "I consider both you and pa extremely uncharitable to indulge in such suspicions. I have seen a good deal more of the Count than either of you, and he is a delightful man."

"Well, don't waste your time disputing, girls," interrupted Mrs. Dinsmore, " you have yet to decide what you will wear to-night."

They were in the dressing-room appropriated to the sisters during their stay; Mildred was with them, Mrs. Dinsmore having invited her in, that they might have the benefit of her taste.

A quantity of finery was spread out upon the bed, table, and chairs, and presently the four were deep in consultation on the all important subject.

Mildred was gifted with artistic taste in dress, and great facility in giving form and shape to her conceptions, by the use of scissors and needle. She was also very obliging, and having fallen to-day into the hands of those who were selfishly unscrupulous about imposing upon good nature, she was given little rest until the two girls were fully attired for the ball.

They surveyed themselves with delight; and indeed both looked remarkably well for them; Juliet in white gauze over pale blue silk, and a few white blossoms from the greenhouse in her hair; Reba in black silk with black lace overskirt looped with scarlet ribbons, and hair trimmed with flowers of the same brilliant hue.

She was in her wildest spirits, dancing, and pirouetting round the room, declaring that Mildred had laid her under lasting obligations, she had had no idea how handsome she was, and it would be strange if she didn't make a conquest before the evening was over; Juliet hearing it all with a half contemptuous smile, while contemplating the reflection of her own charms in the glass, with the self-satisfied thought that they far exceeded those of her sister.

"You are entirely welcome," said Mildred, "and I am very glad you are satisfied with the result of my labors. Now I must go to Aunt Belle, for I promised to put the finishing touches to her toilet."

"We'll go too, and show ourselves," said Reba, and all three tripped gayly down the stairs, into Mrs. Dinsmore's dressing-room.

They found her resplendent in silk, lace and diamonds. The costly gems depended from her ears, sparkled on her wrists, at her throat, on every link of her watch chain; and Mildred's task was to place a spray of them in her hair, already elaborately dressed by her waiting maid.

"Oh, you are splendid, Aunt Belle!" cried Reba, clapping her hands "I declare I believe you look younger and prettier than either of us."

"Don't turn flatterer, child," said Mrs Dinsmore, coloring with pleasure at the compliment, and giving her mirror a glance of unmistakable satisfaction.

"Oh, you needn't pretend you don't know it," laughed Reba. "But now look at us and say if you're not proud of your nieces."

"Yes indeed," Mrs. Dinsmore said after a moment's critical survey, "you are charming girls, both of you. Mildred, I think you deserve any amount of credit."

"Eh! what has she been about?" Mr. Dinsmore asked, coming in from an adjoining room; "superintending the toilet of these girls? Why she is certainly a young lady of taste, and a useful member of society."

"Decidedly prettier in her neat home dress than they in all their finery," he added mentally. Then aloud, "Come, Milly, don't you begin to want to go along? It isn't too late yet to change your mind. We'll wait for you to dress"

"Thank you," she answered brightly, "but I have not changed my mind, and really feel quite sure that I shall enjoy myself better at home."

"Such odd taste," laughed Reba.

"But perhaps she does not expect to pass the time alone," drawled Juliet with a significant look.

Mildred repelled the insinuation with dignity. "I expect no company but my books," she said, "and certainly desire no other."

She was entirely sincere, yet it did seem a little lonely as she sat by the fire in her own room after they had gone.

But she turned resolutely to her books, soon grew interested, and after a couple of hours spent in close study, retired to bed.

Only her uncle, Miss Worth, and the children met her at the breakfast-table the next morning.

Mr. Dinsmore explained that his wife and her nieces were sleeping off their fatigue, adding, "The girls danced all night, and really it was near sunrise when we reached home."

"They must be very tired," Mildred said, "Aunt Belle and you too, uncle."

"Yes; I think your plan was the wisest, after all. But what shall you do with yourself to-day? I fear you will be left quite to your own resources."

"I assure you I will be at no loss," she returned with a cheery smile.

The first thing in order after breakfast was

a ride, in which Adelaide, Louise and Lora were her companions. A very enjoyable one, the morning being bright, clear and not very cold.

On their return, as they cantered up the avenue, Adelaide exclaimed, "There's the Ion carriage at the door. What an early call Mrs. Travilla is making!"

But it was only a servant with a note for Mildred; an urgent invitation to her to drive over to Ion and spend the day.

"I send my carriage for you," wrote Mrs. Travilla, "hoping it may not return empty. Uncle Eben is a careful driver, will bring you safely, I think, and carry you back when you feel that your visit must come to an end. I should drive over for you myself, but am confined to the house by a severe cold."

No more welcome invitation could have come to Mildred. Full of delight she hastened to her room to change her riding habit for something more suitable for the occasion. That was the work of but a few moments, and leaving a message for Mrs. Dinsmore, who had not risen, she was presently bowling briskly along the road leading to Ion.

She anticipated a delightful day and was not disappointed. It was passed principally in Mrs. Travilla's boudoir and without other companionship, and seemed to Mildred very much like a day at home with her mother; for this new friend was a woman of the same spirit, and very similar gifts and graces. And she received her young guest with truly motherly warmth and tenderness of greeting.

The talk was first of Mildred's far off home and the dear ones there, then of the better land and the dearest Friend of all that either possessed; and while conversing of Him and His wondrous love their hearts were drawn very close together.

"Mrs. Travilla," Mildred said, breaking a pause in the conversation, "there is some one I want you to help me pray for; one who wants just such a kind, loving, powerful, everpresent Friend as Jesus."

"Yes, my child, I will," Mrs. Travilla responded with feeling, "we will unite our prayers, and he will know whom we mean, though I am ignorant of it; He whose precious promise is, 'If two of you shall agree on earth as touching anything that they shall ask it shall be done of them of my Father which is in heaven.'"

"It *is* a precious promise," Mildred said, tears springing to her eyes. "And there are others—O, Mrs. Travilla, can you not guess

whom ? that I want to plead it for. Some
that I love, whc are very kind to me, but seem
to care nothing at all about this Friend, and to
have no thought or concern for anything beyond this life."

"Yes, I know," Mrs. Travilla said, pressing
the girl's hand tenderly in hers, " and you may
well believe that I have not known them all
these years without often asking my dear Lord
to reveal himself to them in all his loveliness ;
and now I am very, very glad to have a helper
in this."

They sat silent then for some minutes,
when the adornments of the room attracting
Mildred's eye, reminded her of a question she
had been longing to ask.

Beginning with an account of her visit to
Mrs. Landreth and the talk between them,
in which Mrs. Travilla seemed interested, she
went on to say, with a smiling glance around
the tasteful apartment, "I feel sure that you
do not think as she does, and that she is not
right in her views or practice either ; and yet
I confess I am at a loss to know how to refute
her arguments. So I have wanted to ask an
explanation of your views. Do you think Mrs
Landreth a really good Christian woman ?"

"Yes, my dear, I do," Mrs. Travilla said

" She is beyond question very self-denying and benevolent ; but I think she forgets that we are to ' *adorn* the doctrine of God our Saviour in al things ; ' and so fails to recommend it as she might to others ; particularly her husband and his nephew.

" I quite agree with your mother that it is a wife's duty to study the comfort and happiness of her husband in everything that she can without violating the plain commands of God.

" Mrs. Landreth and I take different views on the question of the best way to help the poor. She gives money, I let them earn it, paying them liberally for their work ; this plan encourages industry and honest pride of independence ; while the other teaches them to be willing to be idle pensioners on the bounty of their richer neighbors.

" Mine certainly seems the more self-indulgent way," she added with a smile, " for my house is thus filled with pretty things while Mrs. Landreth's is left very bare of ornament and yet I think it is the better plan."

" I am sure it is," Mildred responded with an energy and positiveness that brought a musical laugh from the lips of her friend.

" And," resumed Mrs. Travilla, " we differ quite as decidedly on the question of dress—she considering it a duty to spend as little as possible upon herself, that she may have the more to give; I thinking that those who have the means to do so without stinting their charities, or driving hard bargains with their tradesmen, should buy beautiful and expensive things in order to help and encourage manufacturers, and render themselves and their houses attractive.

"Surely God would not have implanted in us so strong a love of the beautiful, and given so much to gratify it, if he meant us to ignore and repress it."

"No, surely not," Mildred said, thoughtfully. "Oh, how good he is! how much he has given us to enjoy! there are so many beautiful sights and sounds in nature, so much to gratify the taste and smell—the perfume from your plants comes most pleasantly to my nostrils at this moment, and the sweet song of that mocking bird to my ear. And I do so love old ocean's roar and the rippling of running water. Does it not seem like a slander upon the God of love, to teach that he would have us spend all our time, effort and means on those things that are utilitarian only?"

"It certainly does; and yet are not some of these things which some condemn as mere indulgences, really useful, after all? the surround ings affect the spirits, and they in turn the health, and therefore the ability to work Grand or beautiful scenery has often an inspiring or soothing effect, and their pictured representations the same to some extent."

"And just so with a sweet and noble face," Mildred said, "and what a lovely one that is," turning her eyes toward a painting on the opposite wall.

"Yes," returned her friend, "I love to lie on my couch and gaze upon it, when not able to sit up, and it has been a comfort and help to me in many an hour of pain or sadness. Ah who shall say that an artist's work is a waste of time—when his pencil is devoted to the reproduction of the good and beautiful—or that his God-given talent is not to be improved?"

Then she drew Mildred's attention to other paintings, and pieces of fancy work, to each of which she had a story attached: generally of a struggle with poverty and want on the part of the one of whose talent and skill it was a specimen.

These tales were told in no boastful spirit yet Mildred learned from them a valuable lesson on the best use of wealth, and how much good might be done with it, in the way of lending a helping hand to those who needed assist ance or lift them out of otherwise hopeless poverty, and how it could be accomplished without sacrificing a praiseworthy pride of independence.

Chapter Twelfth.

"O credulity,
Security's blind nurse, the dream of fools."

MASON.

MRS. DINSMORE carried out her plan of filling her house with company during the holidays.
They were mostly young people, and the time
was spent in a constant round of festivities.

In these Mildred bore some share; for she
thought it right that she should do her part in
entertaining her aunt's guests. Nor did her
conscience forbid innocent recreation at proper
times and seasons, though she could not consent to make mere amusement the business of
her life.

Some half dozen or more of the neighboring
gentry were invited for the whole fortnight,
while others came for an evening, a day, or two
or three days, and on Christmas Eve and New
Year's night, large parties were given.

It was on the latter occasion that Mildred

noticed among the guests, for the first time, a handsome man, apparently about thirty years of age, who was an entire stranger to her.

His broadcloth and linen were of the finest, a magnificent solitaire diamond adorned the little finger of his right hand; he wore an imperial and heavy moustache, and something foreign in his look and·manner, as well as the fact that he seemed to be paying assiduous court to Juliet, suggested to Mildred the probability that he was the Count De Lisle, of whom she had heard her make such frequent mention.

She was not long left in doubt as to that, for the next moment Reba whispered his name in her ear, adding "Juliet is in the seventh heaven, of course."

" There is something sinister in the expression of his face," thought Mildred, turning away. "I do not like it. Yet it is strangely familiar too. Where can I possibly have seen it before?"

His attention had been attracted to her and he inquired of Juliet, "Who is that pretty girl in pink and white!"

"Pretty!" returned Miss Marsden with a scornful toss of the head. "I cannot say that I admire her style. She's a Miss Keith, a sort of far away niece of Uncle Dinsmore : a Northern girl and poor, I imagine; for her father's a country lawyer with a large family."

Juliet was absolutely ignorant of Mr. Keith's circumstances, but it suited her plans to make it appear that she was no heiress; quite her own inferior in the matter of wealth, whatever she might be in looks.

"Do not be offended, my angel," he whispered bending over her and speaking with a slightly foreign accent which she had again and again extolled to Reba as "perfectly delicious," "I meant not that she was half so beautiful or charmant as yourself."

"Ah, Count, you are a sad flatterer," she returned with a simper.

"No, no! pardon the contradiction, Miss Juliet, but de truth is nefer flattery."

"A penny for your thoughts, Miss Keith," said a voice at Mildred's side.

"Ah, good evening, Mr. Landreth," she answered turning toward the speaker. "You are welcome to them gratis. I am wondering where I have seen Miss Marsden's admirer before to-night, or if it is only a resemblance, real or fancied, to some one else that I see in him."

"1 cannot tell, indeed," he said, furtively watching the man for a moment, "but there is something in his face that would make me sorry to see him ingratiating himself with a lady friend of mine."

"Excuse me, but I must ask you to move, as we are going to dance and want this sofa behind you, put out of the way," said Reba, coming up to them with two servants.

"Certainly," Mildred said, taking Mr. Landreth's offered arm.

They passed down the room and out into the conservatory beyond.

"Are you engaged for the first set?" he asked.

"No; nor for any other," she answered with a smile. "I do not dance, Mr. Landreth."

"It is not too late to begin," he remarked persuasively.

"No, it is too soon."

"You don't think it wrong?" he queried as in surprise, "here in your home as it were? It is different, is it not, from attending a ball?"

"Yes; but I might grow so fond of it as to want to go to balls. I think it safest for me to avoid the temptation."

Sets were forming as they returned to the drawing-room, and Miss Worth, who had been sent for, to play the piano, was just entering by another door.

She had kept apart from the guests, spending almost all her time in her own room; so that Mildred had seen very little of her for some days past.

She noticed on the instant of her entrance, that she was looking pale and worn; then that her pallor suddenly increased to ghastliness, as on stepping in, she came face to face with Juliet and the Count in the nearest set, standing side by side.

He, too, started slightly and turned pale for a moment as his eyes met those of the governess; but neither spoke and pushing hastily past him she sat down at the instrument.

She felt herself reeling in her seat and thought she should fall to the floor; everything seemed to be turning round : but conquering her emotion by a great effort, she ran her fingers over the keys and dashed off into a lively dancing tune.

Her head was in a whirl, a mist swam before her eyes so that she could not see the notes, but her fingers flew so fast that the dancers were soon panting for breath in their efforts to keep pace with the music.

"Not so fast! not so fast!" called several voices, but though for an instant she slackened her speed, the next she was rattling on as before

Set after set had been danced, Juliet **and** the count taking part in them all, and now **he** led her panting to a seat.

"I like not zose tunes so well as some other," he remarked. "May I claim ze privilege to speak to ze player zat she choose something else, and not play quite so rapid?"

"Oh yes, certainly," smiled Juliet sweetly.

Miss Worth was turning over her music **in** search of a waltz some one had called for, when a voice spoke at her side; a voice that made her start and shiver, though she did not look round.

"Your execution was von leetle bit **too** rapid for us," it said in an ordinary tone, then in a whisper, the lips close to her ear, "Meet me half an hour after the company disperses; behind the clump of evergreens at the foot of the avenue."

"Yes," she answered, almost under her breath, and without so much as turning her head.

She saw as in a nightmare, a white hand, too large to be a woman's, with a solitaire diamond sparkling on the fourth finger, busied among the sheets of music before her, then it vanished, her strained ear catching the faint echo of the retreating step.

She kept her eyes on her notes, her fingers wandering mechanically over the keys, calling forth low, soft strains of music, while the dancers passed out into the refreshment room. She kept it up unceasingly until they returned; then changed to a waltz in obedience to directions, as couples began taking their places on the floor. How long it lasted she did not know, it seemed an age of suffering to her before she found herself again alone in the solitude of her own room.

As she entered the clock on the mantel struck two. She glanced at it and sank into a chair by the fire.

"Half an hour," she sighed, shivering and crouching over the blaze. "What an age to wait; and yet I'm afraid not long enough to let them all get to bed and asleep. What if I should be seen!"

She dropped her face into her hands with a low groan. It was some minutes before she lifted it again for another glance at the clock; a wan, weary, haggard face, full of dread and distress, but with no tears in the burning eyes.

Slowly the moments dragged themselves along till at last the minute hand pointed to the half hour, when she rose, wrapped herself in a large dark shawl, putting it over her head, listened at her door for a moment, to make sure that all was quiet, then glided softly down the stairs, let herself out at a back door, and creeping along close to the wall of the house, then in the shadow of the trees that lined the avenue, gained at length the clump of evergreens at its farther end.

A biting north wind swept the hard, frozen ground, and rustled the dry leaves at her feet, as she stood leaning against a tree in an intensely listening attitude. It seemed to pierce to her very vitals, and shuddering and trembling with the cold, and nervous dread, she drew the shawl more closely about her, while straining her eyes through the gloom to catch a glimpse of him whom she had come to meet; for there was no light save that shining in the winter sky.

She had waited but a moment, when a stealthy step drew near, and a tall form wrapped in a cloak, stood before her.

" Here first ?" he said in a cautious whisper.

"Yes," she answered, in the same low key, and with a sudden catching of her breath. " Oh, why are you here ?"

" For my own advantage," he answered half defiantly, " and," in a threatening tone, " you'd better have a care how you betray me."

"I have no desire to do so," she returned, with a weary sigh, "but you must go, and at once ; you will ruin me if you stay; you must see that."

"Pooh . I see no such thing. And must is a word you have no right to use to me. Keep your mouth shut, and all will go well."

"What is your object in coming here ?"

"Plain enough, I should think," he answered with a sneer.

"You are deceiving that silly girl, and intend to marry her, simply for her money ?"

"Exactly. Who needs money more than I? "

" And how long will it take you to squander it ?"

" Depends upon how much there is," he returned with a sardonic laugh.

" And your luck at the gaming table, I presume," she said bitterly. " You are acting most dishonorably toward the girl. She would not look at you if she knew—"

" That I am an American born citizen, eh ? Well, am I any the worse for that ? "

" Not for that—not in my esteem ; but you know, you *know* that is not all, nor the worst by a great deal ! " she cried in a tone of suppressed agony. " And you ask me to stand by and see you deceive this girl to her ruin, never

stretching out a finger for her help! I cannot
do it. I will not! Go! go! you must! you
must never show your face here again!"

"Be quiet!" he said angrily; for in her
excitement she had raised her voice to a dan-
gerously high pitch. "And look at home," he
went on: "remember that you are partly responsible for my ruin, and that you, too, are
sailing under false colors."

"But not to the injury of any one; not with
any evil intent," she answered, clasping her
hands beseechingly. "And if you drive me
from here, Harry, you will be taking the bread
out of our mother's mouth. It is surely enough
that you do nothing for her support yourself."

"I'll help with that when I have secured
this girl and her money," he said with an evil
laugh. "Just you keep quiet and all will
go well. Keep my secret, and I'll keep
yours."

She leaned back wearily against the tree,
clasping her hands more tightly over her throbbing heart; tears sprang to her eyes, her lips
trembled, but no sound came from them.

"Well?" he cried impatiently.

"Harry," she said, very low and tremulously, "I have been reading a good deal lately
in an old book—one whose teachings we used

to respect in our innocent childhood—and it tells me that 'the way of transgressors is hard;' that though 'hand join in hand, the wicked shall not be unpunished'; that there is such a thing as sinning away your day of grace; and it says, 'Seek ye the Lord while he may be found, call ye upon him while he is near.' O, Harry, turn from your wicked ways before it is forever too late. There is mercy even for you, if you will turn now."

Spell-bound with astonishment, he had heard her thus far in absolute silence; but now he interrupted her with a savage oath.

"I didn't know you'd turned pious," he sneered. "And I didn't come here to be preached to. If you know what's for your good you'll keep quiet; that's all I have to say. And now I'm off. I can't stand here catching my death of cold."

He was turning away, but she grasped a fold of his cloak.

"Harry," she said in a choking voice, "we used to be fond of each other: I was very proud of my handsome brother; and—and we've been parted for five years!"

"That's true, Gerty," he said in a softened tone, turning back and throwing an arm about her waist; let's kiss and be friends."

"Harry," she whispered, clinging to him, "do you know anything of—of *him?*"

"No; and don't want to!" he answered savagely. "You're not fool enough to care for him now?"

"Women are fools," was all she said in reply.

And they parted; he disappearing in the direction of the road, she creeping back to the house, and regaining the shelter of her room; fortunately without meeting any one on the way.

She was tired, oh, *so* tired! her strength scarcely sufficient to bring her to the desired haven; but even there she could not rest. She did not undress or lie down, but crouched beside the fire, her hands clasped about her knees, her head bowed upon her breast, while the monotonous ticking of the clock told off the weary seconds, and the smouldering embers burned out leaving nothing but the cold ashes on the hearth.

Chapter Thirteenth.

"In desert wilds, in midnight gloom,
In grateful joy, in trying pain,
In laughing youth, or nigh the tomb,
Ah ! when is prayer unheard or vain ?"

ELIZA COOK.

THE cold, grey dawn of the winter morning
was stealing in at the windows as at last, sighing heavily, the governess lifted her head with
a returning consciousness of her surroundings.

How dreary it all looked, in the dim, uncertain light ! the disordered room, the fireless
hearth—fit emblem, as it seemed, of the cold,
almost dead heart within her.

Life was like a desert at that moment, a
rough, weary road where thorns and briars constantly pierced her tired feet. Why should
she stay ? Why not lie down and rest in a
quiet grave ?

She rose slowly, stiff from the constrained
posture, and dragged herself across the room.
Opening her wardrobe door, she took from the

shelf a vial labelled "laudanum." She held it
a moment in her hand.

"It is only to go to sleep," she said, half
aloud, "to go to sleep, and never wake again.
Never? ah! if I could be sure, *sure* of that!"

"'And the smoke of their torment ascend-
eth up forever and ever.' 'Where their worm
dieth not, and the fire is not quenched.'"

With a shudder, she put it hastily back,
locked the door, and threw herself upon the bed.

"Oh, God, forgive me!" she cried, "keep
me, keep me, or I shall do it yet! And then—
forever and ever! No space for repentance, no
coming back!"

At length tired nature found temporary relief in the heavy, dreamless slumber of utter
exhaustion.

Hours passed, and still she slept on, hearing
not, nor heeding the sounds of returning life in
the household.

They were very late after their long night of
revelry; breakfast was not on the table till ten
o'clock, and even then no one answered the summons but the master of the house and Mildred.

The children had taken their morning meal
two hours before.

"An unexpected pleasure, this, Milly, my
dear," was Mr. Dinsmore's greeting.

"What, uncle, you did not surely expect me to be still in bed!"

"Well no; but I thought you would be looking fagged and worn; instead of which, your face is fresh and fair as a rose just washed with dew, and bright as the morning."

"And why not, if sufficient rest will do it?" she returned, laughingly. "I retired at twelve, and had my eight hours of sound, refreshing sleep."

"Ah, you are a wise little woman! too sensible to let late hours rob you of health and good looks, and make you old before your time. What is it Solomon says? 'Early to bed and early to rise?'"

"O, uncle, what a joke! there no use in your pretending that you don't know any better than that," she answered merrily.

"Well, perhaps I do; but he certainly says something about lying late in bed."

"Several things; one occurs to me now. Love not sleep, lest thou come to poverty; open thine eyes, and thou shalt be satisfied with bread.' But it cannot mean that we should not take needful rest?"

"Oh no, of course not! there's nothing gained by that. But where's Miss Worth!"

"She has not joined us since the house has

been so full of guests. I think she takes her meals with the children in the nursery."

" Ah, yes; I presume so; but I had forgotten it, and it struck me that she might be ill. I thought she was looking badly last night. Did you notice it ?"

" Yes; I did. I will inquire about her," Mildred said, remembering with a pang of self-reproach how ghastly a face the governess had worn on taking her seat at the piano.

She might be very ill, unable to call for help, neglected by the sleepy maids, and she herself had been up for two hours and ought to have gone to her door to inquire.

She went immediately on leaving the table, her alarm and anxiety increased on the way thither by the information, gleaned from one of the servants, that Miss Worth had not been present at the nursery breakfast.

Mildred rapped lightly, then louder, and receiving no answer, tried the door. It opened and she stole softly in.

Miss Worth lay on the outside of the bed, still dressed as she had last seen her—in the drawing room at the piano—and sleeping heavily. Her face was very pale and distressed and she moaned now and then as if in pain.

She had nothing over her; but a heavy

dark shawl lay on the floor beside the chimney Mildred picked it up and spread it over her, drew down the blinds to shut out the glare of the sun, rang for the maid, and while waiting for her, moved quietly about the room putting things in their places.

"It is very cold here, for the fire is quite out and must be made up at once," she whispered, meeting the girl at the door and motioning her to make no noise. "Go bring up wood and kindling."

"De governess sick, Miss Milly?" queried the servant, sending a curious glance in the direction of the bed.

"I don't know, Dinah, perhaps only tired, for she was up very late last night; but she is asleep and must not be disturbed." And Mildred motioned her imperatively away.

It was not till an hour later that Miss Worth stirred and woke to find a cheerful fire blazing on the hearth and Mildred beside it quietly knitting.

She put down her work hastily, rose and came forward as she perceived the governess's eyes fixed upon her in a sort of perplexed surprise.

"Excuse the intrusion," Mildred said; "but I thought you seemed ill, and was afraid you

might need help. I hope your sleep has refreshed you, and that you will let me order the
breakfast they are keeping hot for you in the
kitchen."

"Thank you, I cannot understand such kindness to me," Miss Worth said huskily. "I was
very tired—not sick, I think—and I suppose
the sleep has done me good."

"And you will eat something ? "

"I will try, since you are so good."

The effort was but indifferently successful,
yet Miss Worth steadily refused to acknowledge
herself on the sick list, and insisted that she
was able to work and must do so ; and Mildred
went away, feeling troubled and anxious.

Left alone, Miss Worth took out her writing materials, then resting her elbows on the
table, her face in her hands, sat thus for a long
time without moving, a heavy sigh now and
then escaping her.

At last she took up her pen and wrote
rapidly for several minutes, then snatching up
the paper, she tore it into fragments and threw
them into the fire.

Another sheet shared the same fate, and
seemingly giving it up in despair, she rose and
walked the floor.

"Oh. if I only knew what to do, what to

say!" she moaned. "If he would but hear reason; if he would but forsake his evil courses! And yet!—Oh, if I had a friend! just one wise, true friend to advise and help me! But I dare not breathe my terrible fears to any mortal; and who is there that would care to listen?"

Her eye fell on the Bible lying there on the table, and with the sight came the recollection of the texts Mildred had quoted to her.

She almost heard a gentle, tender voice saying "Come unto me—and I will give you rest," and falling on her knees she cried to him,

"Lord Jesus I do come! I give myself to thee; and oh, I beseech thee in thy great mercy and loving kindness to help me in this my hour of perplexity and distress!"

Strange what a blessed calm succeeded the storm. She rose from her knees wondrously soothed and quieted. She had found a Friend who had pledged His word to help her and who had all power in heaven and in earth. What need she fear? "If God be for us, who can be against us?"

There might be trouble in store for her — great and sore trouble—but He would help her through.

There was a sound of gay young voices in

the halls without and on the stairway; a carriage had driven to the door, an open barouche, and presently she saw it going down the avenue and that Mr. and Mrs. Dinsmore and the three young ladies were in it.

The older children were away from home, as she knew, spending a few days at a neighboring plantation; the younger ones were probably in the nursery.

She watched the carriage till it was lost to sight far down the road, then was turning from the window, with the thought in her mind that it would be a blessing to Juliet Marsden, as well as herself, if it were taking her home to her father's care, when she caught sight of a horseman coming from the opposite direction.

She stood still, scanning him narrowly as he turned in at the gate and came cantering up the avenue; as he drew near she recognized him with a start of surprise—terror mingling with it at first, but changing instantly to joy that he had assuredly missed the object of his visit.

It was her scoundrel brother; yet spite of all the distress and anguish of mind he was causing her, she was conscious of a thrill of sisterly pride in his handsome face and form, and the grace and ease of his horsemanship.

But she must seize this unhoped-for opportunity; there were motives she could urge
which escaped her thoughts the previous night,
and that might, perhaps, have weight with
him; and much now depended upon prompt
action on her part.

She flew down the stairs and admitted him
herself, before he had had time to ring; and
fortunately no servant had perceived his approach.

He looked at her in extreme surprise.

"How is this?" he inquired, with an ill-
natured sneer, "have you been promoted to the
office of porter?"

"Hush!" she answered, in an imperative
whisper. "Come in here;" and she led the
way into a little parlor close at hand.

"Excuse the impertinence, Madame, but I
did not come to see you," he said angrily, as he
followed her in.

"I am well aware of that fact," she said in
a calm tone of quiet firmness, as she turned and
faced him. "Nevertheless, I believe I am the
one, and the only one you will see; and it is
well, for I have something of importance to
say."

"Where is Miss Marsden?" he demanded.

"Gone for a drive, and all the other ladies

with her; Mr. Dinsmore also. The last of the
guests left an hour since, and we may chat for
a good while without much fear of interruption."

"Suppose I don't choose," he returned,
straightening himself with a defiant air.

"Harry, you must hear me!" she said, laying a detaining hand upon his arm, for he was
moving toward the door.

"That's a strong word, and one you've no
right to use to me," he answered moodily, yet
yielding to her determined will.

She pointed to a chair, and he sat down.

"Speak and be done with it," he said.

Tears sprang to her eyes, but she forced
them back.

"Are you mad, Harry, that you venture a
return to this country?" she asked in an undertone, her voice trembling with excitement,
"can you have forgotten the danger that hangs
over you?"

"It's trifling, considering the changes five
years have made," he said, with affected non-
chalance; but his cheek paled.

"Don't deceive yourself, don't trust to that;
I recognized you at the first glance," she said,
with the earnestness of one determined to con
vince.

"Well, one of my own family would, of course, be more apt to do so than any one else. And I was never known in this part of the country."

"No; but people travel about a great deal; Northerners come South frequently; especially in winter; and you may, any day, come face to face with some old acquaintance who will recognize you, and have you arrested; and then—" she hid her face and shuddered. "O Harry," she cried, "I shall live in terror till I know you are safe on the other side of the ocean."

"I'll go in all haste when I have secured my prize," he said coldly.

"Give it up," she entreated, "you have no right to drag an innocent girl down to infamy with you. Better go and make an honest living by the labor of your hands."

"I wasn't brought up to that, and infinitely prefer to live by my wits," he answered, with an evil smile, "and they'll have to help me to the means to pay my passage to those foreign shores you so highly recommend."

"Sell this: it would surely bring more than enough for that," she said, pointing to the glittering gem on his finger.

"Paste, my dear, nothing but paste," he laughed. ' Clever imitation, isn't it?"

"Ah, Harry, a fair type of its owner, 1 fear," she said sorrowfully.

"Thanks for the compliment," he answered with a bitter laugh.   "Well, after all, it *is a* compliment, taken in the sense that I'm as clever an imitation of what Miss Marsden takes me for, as this is of a real diamond; and perhaps she's as good a judge of the first article, as you are of the other; ha! ha!"

"Harry," cried his sister, "are you utterly heartless? have you no pity at all for that poor silly girl?"

"Pooh! Gertrude, I have to look out for myself; and other people must do the same; I tell you it is a case of necessity," he answered doggedly.

"No," she said, "there cannot be a necessity for wrong doing, and if persisted in it must end at last in terrible retribution; both in this world and the next," she added in low, tremulous tones.

"I'll risk it," he said with an oath.   "And as to the girl, why she'd break her silly heart if I should forsake her," he added, with an unpleasant laugh, "You've no idea how deeply in love she is."

"You are mistaken: she has no heart to break, and loves nobody, half so well as herself.

She will never be the woman to stand by and comfort you in adversity : therefore you will be doing a foolish thing to make her your wife, even though you consult your own interest alone."

At that he only laughed, saying that as the girl's money was all he wanted, he didn't care whether she stood by him or not after he once got it into his possession.

She renewed her warnings and entreaties, urging every motive she could think of to induce him to give up his wicked designs upon Juliet Marsden, and forsake all his evil courses; but in vain; his heart was fully set in him to do evil, and neither love of his mother and sisters, nor pity for the deluded girl, could move him.

Nor did fear of punishment deter him. He was no coward, he said, glorying in his shame, and showing himself utterly devoid of wisdom ' for the fear of the Lord, that is wisdom ; and to depart from evil, is understanding ;' and the Bible calls those fools who make a mock at sin, despise instruction and hate to depart from evil.

At length there was a sound of approaching wheels ; upon which he exclaimed in a relieved tone, "There, you'd better go ; it won't help either you or me for us to be caught together."

"No," she assented, rising hastily, "1 must go.   O, Harry, think of what I've been saying and don't rush headlong to destruction!"

"There! I've had enough of it!" he retorted angrily.   "I'll do as I please.   And do you keep yourself quiet."

Chapter Fourteenth.

"How poor a thing is pride!"

"The beauty you o'erprise so, time or sickness
Can change to loath'd deformity; your wealth
The prey of thieves.'

—MASSINGER.

THE most open-handed hospitality having
ever been the rule at Roselands, it was no difficult matter for Count De Lisle to get himself
invited to stay to tea and spend the evening;
in fact it was long past midnight when he at
last took leave of Juliet and went away.

The thud of his horse's hoofs as he galloped
down the avenue, brought a pale, haggard face
to an upper window; but the dim light of the
stars revealed nothing save the merest outline
of the steed and his rider, and that for but an
instant.

The watcher turned away, sighing to herself,
"I cannot see him, but it must be he," hastily
crossed the room and stole noiselessly into the
hall beyond.

The hours spent by him in dalliance with

Juliet (they had had the drawing-room to themselves since ten o'clock) had been to her—his
much tried sister—a time of bitter anguish and
fierce mental conflict.

How could she permit this wickedness?
yet how prevent it, when the only way to do
so was by exposing him—her brother?

It seemed a terribly hard thing to do, for
she loved him, and his disgrace was hers, and
that of the whole family.

She was sorely tempted to leave Juliet to
the fate she seemed to be drawing upon herself
by her egregious folly,—that of becoming the
wife of a spendthrift, and one whose vices had
led him to commit a crime against the laws of
the land, the penalty of which was a term of
years in the penitentiary.

It would be a sad fate, but perhaps not un-
deserved by a girl who would rush into it in
opposition to the known wishes and commands
of her parents.

Harry had unguardedly admitted to his sister that he had no hope of winning the consent
of either Mr. or Mrs. Marsden ; that they were,
in fact, so violently opposed to his suit, that he
dared not visit their daughter in her own home ;
but he had exultingly added that he was perfectly certain of his ability to persuade Juliet

to elope with him, and meant to do so sooner or later.

Well, should he accomplish that, and escape to Europe with his prize, his family probably would not suffer any ill consequence. No one here knew his real name, or had the slightest suspicion that Miss Worth was in any way connected with him; but she felt morally certain that in case Mrs. Dinsmore discovered the truth, her situation at Roselands was lost; she would be sent away without a recommendation; then it might be months before she could get employment elsewhere, and that meant beggary to herself, and those nearest and dearest to her.

Surely no motive of self-interest urged her to stretch out a hand to save Juliet Marsden from falling into the snare spread for her unwary feet. Yet pity for the girl, a strong sense of justice, and more than all, a desire to do the will of her new found Friend, prevailed over all selfish considerations, and she fully determined to give the warning, though in a way to risk as little as possible, and for the last half hour she had watched and waited for the opportunity.

Juliet came up the stairs with a light, quick step, and as she passed underneath the lamp swung from the ceiling, its rays, falling full

upon her, gave to Miss Worth a moment's dis
tinct view of her face.

It wore an expression of exultant joy; the
cheeks were flushed, the eyes glittering, the lips
smiling.

"He has offered himself and been ac
cepted," was Miss Worth's conclusion; "there
is no time to be lost;" and stepping forward,
she stood directly in Juliet's path, confronting
her with calm, pale face, and determined air.

"What is the meaning of this?" asked Juliet, recoiling, and regarding the governess with
mingled anger and hauteur, "Will you be good
enough to step aside, and allow me to pass on
to my own apartments?"

"Excuse me, Miss Marsden, but I must have
a word with you," returned the person addressed, in low, distinct tones, and not moving
a hair's breadth from the position she had
taken.

"Indeed!" was the scornful rejoinder,
"and pray, who may you be that take such airs
upon yourself? My aunt's governess, if I am
not mistaken, a person with whom I can have
nothing in common. Keep your communica-
tions for those in your own station in life.
Will you step out of my way?"

"Not yet; not till I have discharged my

duty to you, Miss Marsden, I must speak a word of warning; I cannot see you rushing headlong to destruction without crying out to you to beware; and I have no motive for doing so but pity for you."

Juliet's astonishment was unbounded. What could the creature mean? What indeed, but to insult her.

"Pity for me!" she cried with withering scorn, "you, a poor dependent governess, pity me! me the daughter of a wealthy Kentucky planter and an heiress in my own right. Keep your compassion for such as want it, I will none of it!" and she would have pushed past Miss Worth, but the latter laid a hand on her arm, not roughly but with determination.

"It is of Count De Lisle I would speak to you," she said almost under her breath. "No, I call that back; for he has no right to either the name or the title."

"How dare you!" cried Juliet with flashing eyes, shaking off the detaining hand and drawing herself up to her full height. "What do you know of him?"

"Far more than you do," returned the other calmly. "I have known him all his life and I tell you he is not what you suppose—not what he gives himself out to be;—but a man with

out fortune or title—an American by birth and
education, and seeking you merely for your
wealth."

"I don't believe a word of it! It's all a
pack of lies that you have invented because you
are envious of me. Stand out of my way and
don't presume to speak to me again on this subject, nor any other."

So saying the angry girl swept proudly past
the humble governess, whom she regarded as a
menial and an impertinent meddler in her
affairs, and gaining her apartments, shut and
locked herself in with a noise that roused her
sleeping sister.

"The impudent creature!" she muttered.

"Who?" queried Reba, starting up in bed.
"Have you actually discovered that pa is right
and your count a mercenary adventurer?"

"Nonsense! no; I've learned no such
thing!"

"What then? who is the impudent creature you are anathematizing?"

"Aunt Belle's governess. She actually
waylaid me in the hall and forced me to stand
still and listen while she uttered a warning
against him, pretending that he was an old acquaintance of hers. I shall complain to aunt and
have her turned adrift for her impertinence."

"Better not," laughed Reba; "'twould only tend to rouse suspicion against him. It must be very late; I advise you to wake up your maid and get ready for bed."

The encounter had left Miss Worth in quite as unamiable a frame of mind as that of her antagonist; for the insulting arrogance of Juliet's manner had sorely wounded her pride; it was hard to take such treatment from one who was her superior in nothing but the accident of wealth, and in fact decidedly inferior in the higher gifts of intellect and education.

"I wash my hands of the whole affair; I will leave her to her fate," Miss Worth said to herself as she turned in at her own door again and secured it after her.

With that she endeavored to dismiss the whole matter from her mind; she was exceedingly weary and must have rest, and presently everything was forgotten in a heavy, dreamless sleep.

But with the first moment of wakefulness the burden again pressed heavily. She could not be indifferent to her brother's wrong-doing nor to the danger of his discovery, arrest and punishment for his former crime.

But the holidays were over and she must return to her duties in the schoolroom; perhaps

it was well for her that it was so, since it com
pelled her to give her thoughts to other subjects

Still taking her meals in the nursery, she
saw nothing of the lady guests till Mildred came
in the afternoon with a recitation.

Mildred was quietly and steadily pursuing
the course of study which she had laid out for
herself; mingling to some extent in the employ-
ments and pastimes of those about her, but con-
triving to retire betimes almost every night,
and by early rising to secure the morning hours
for the improvement of her mind; a season safe
from interruption by her aunt and her nieces,
as it was always spent by them in bed.

In fact there was so utter an absence of
congeniality between Mildred and the other
two girls that they were generally better content to remain apart. And as Mrs. Dinsmore
preferred the companionship of her own nieces,
because of both the ties of kindred and harmony
of taste and feeling, Mildred was left to follow
her own inclinations with little hindrance
from them.

But though continuing her studies, Mildred,
because she felt that the governess was entitled
to the full benefit of the holiday rest, had not,
during the past two weeks, gone to her for assistance or with recitations.

She was glad that she might now do so with propriety; for since the episode of the previous morning she had not been able to forget Miss Worth s pale, distressed countenance; and was really very anxious about her.

She felt quite sure there was some deeper trouble than mere physical pain, and had a longing desire to give sympathy and relief; a desire untainted by a touch of prying curiosity, and that strengthened so greatly during this afternoon's interview that she was fain to give expression to it; doing so with extreme delicacy and tact.

It was when the business part of their interview was over, and Mildred had closed her books and risen to leave the room.

For a moment Miss Worth was silent, her features working with emotion.

" You are very kind," she said at last. " I wish I might confide fully in you, but you are so young: too young and free from care to understand my—"

She broke off abruptly and with a groan, dropped her face upon her folded arms, on the table at which they had been sitting.

" Perhaps so," Mildred said in gently compassionate tones; " I could almost wish for your sake that I were older."

Miss Worth lifted her head, and with almost startling suddenness, and a feverish eagerness in her tones, asked, " Miss Mildred, where is Miss Juliet Marsden to-day ? "

" She has passed the greater part of it in bed, I believe," Mildred answered in utter surprise

" Has—has her lover been here since—since he left her last night ? "

" The Count ? No."

" Can you tell me if she is to go out to-night ? and where ? and who is to be her escort ? Ah, I see you are wondering at my curiosity and it is only natural that you should ; but believe me, it is not the idle inquisitiveness it must seem to you," she went on rapidly and in anguished accents ; " for I have a reason ; there is much at stake—I—I have tried to be indifferent—to say to myself that it is nothing to me if—if that vain, silly girl should meet with the fate her folly deserves ; but I cannot ; I must try to save her—and him.   Oh, if I could but save *him*."

And again she hid her face, while sobs shook her from head to foot.

" Him !" Mildred cried in increased amazement, " what is he to you ?   No, no, I do not ask that.   I have no wish to pry into your secrets "

Miss Worth lifted her head, and wiped away her tears.

"Thank you, for withdrawing that question," she said in a broken voice, "I cannot answer it; but—but this much I will tell you in the strictest confidence. I have known him in other days, and he is not what he professes to be; and it would be ruin, *ruin* to her!"

"Is that so?" Mildred said, with a startled look. "Then surely you will warn her?"

"I have done so, Miss Keith, though it was like drawing my eye teeth to do it; but my sacrifice was unappreciated, my motives were misconstrued; I was treated with scorn and contempt, and have said to myself, 'I have a just right to be angry and indignant, and shall leave her to her fate.'"

"But you will tell my uncle? He might be able to prevent the mischief by setting a watch upon them, and forbidding the man the house."

"No, no, I cannot betray him!" cried Miss Worth in a startled, terrified tone, "and you—you will respect my confidence, Miss Keith?"

"Certainly; but—surely you will not suffer Juliet to be sacrificed?"

"I have warned her," returned the gover

ness, co.lly, "and since she refuses to heed, on
her own head be the consequences."

It was Mildred's turn to be troubled and
perplexed   She stood for a moment in anxious
thought.

"Will you not make one more eff rt?" she
said at length. "Would you not save him
from this wrong doing?   May not the consequences be dreadful to him, too? may not her
father take a terrible revenge, as men sometimes
do on the deceivers and betrayers of their
daughters?"

Miss Worth started, and her wan cheek
turned a shade paler.

"I had not thought of that!" she said,
drawing a long breath. "Oh, what shall I
do?"

They consulted together, but with no more
definite result than a mutual agreement to keep
a strict watch upon the movements of Juliet
and her pseudo nobleman.

Mildred was again about to withdraw, when
Miss Worth stopped her.

"Pardon me, Miss Keith," she said, "but
you have not answered my questions."

"They all go to the theatre to-night, and,
as I happen to know, Mr. Landreth is to escort
Miss Juliet."

"Not the count? but she will meet him there; I am sure of it. You do not go, Miss Mildred?"

"To the theatre! oh, no!"

"Then I must go myself, and watch them."

"Surely that is not necessary," reasoned Mildred, "Uncle, Aunt, Reba—all close at hand."

"Ah! perhaps not," assented the governess, "Possibly it were wiser to leave the task to them."

Mildred went to her room to ponder and pray over the matter, for she was sorely perplexed, and not a little anxious for Juliet.

She asked help and direction for herself and Miss Worth; and that the latter might be led to do her duty, however difficult and painful.

Greatly she wondered what was the tie between her and this spurious count, till it flashed upon her that his familiar look was a strong likeness to the governess. Then she knew it was that of relationship.

Her own duty in the affair formed a serious question in her mind.

Much she wished Miss Worth's communication had not been made in confidence, and that she were free to carry it to her uncle, who

would, in that case, be sure to interfeie effect-
ually to save Ju..iet from falling a prey to the
schemes of this false, designing man.

She could not break her word to the gov
erness, but at length, recalling the fact that she
had heard Reba say her father was suspicious
of Count De Lisle, she determined to repeat that
to her uncle, and thus put him on his guard
against the villain, and his probable plot to in-
veigle Juliet into a clandestine marriage.

It was not a pleasant thing for Mildred to
do; she would much rather not interfere, but
Juliet must be saved at all risks, and neither
she nor Reba had seemed to make a secret of
their father's sentiments.

She went at once in search of Mr. Dinsmore, but learned that he was closeted with a
gentleman on business.   Then a summons
came for her to drive out with her aunt; te^
was ready when they returned; after that she
was occupied with company in the drawing-
room, then in assisting Juliet and Reba to make
their toilet for the evening.

Thus the time slipped by, and when the
carriage had driven away with its load of thea
tre goers, she retired to her own room, without
having had the least opportunity for a word in
private with Mr. Dinsmore.

Chapter Fifteenth.

" It is vain
(I see) to argue 'gainst the grain."
—BUTLER.

JULIET had scarcely taken her seat in Mr. Dinsmore's box when a sweeping glance around the theatre showed her Count De Lisle occupying another at no great distance.

She telegraphed him behind her fan, and during the interval between the first and second acts he joined them.

When Juliet re-entered the carriage which was to convey her home, she carried within her glove, a tiny note written on fine, tinted, highly scented French paper, which he had adroitly slipped into her hand, unobserved by any of her companions.

Under cover of the darkness she transferred it to her bosom, and the first moment that she found herself alone in her dressing-room, it was hastily drawn forth and read at a glance.

Her cheeks flushed, her eyes shone, as with a triumphant smile she refolded and laid it safely by.

On leaving the room to go down to ner late breakfast the next morning, she carried it with her; for not for any consideration would she risk having it seen by other eyes than her own.

She was very late and a good deal flurried in consequence; her thoughts were busy, too, with the important step she had determined to take that night. In her absence of mind she must have been guilty of some carelessness, for on returning to her room, after dawdling for an hour over her meal in company with her aunt and sister, she was horrified to find that the note was missing.

In vain she searched her pockets, shook out the folds of her dress, hunted everywhere, even retracing her steps all the way to the breakfast parlor and looking under and around the table. It was hopelessly lost and she dare not make any ado or inquiry about it.

She was exceedingly fretted and troubled but must conceal her anxiety, only hoping that it had fallen into some place where it would be undiscovered until she and the count had made good their escape from Roselands, and placed themselves beyond successful pursuit.

Fortunately, as she esteemed it, no one had been witness to her perturbation, or her quest, Reba and their aunt having, upon leaving the table, retired together to the boudoir of the latter.

Dire would have been Juliet's anger and alarm could she have known what had actually become of her missing treasure.

Miss Worth, in passing between the school-room and her own apartment, caught sight of a bit of paper lying on the floor at the head of the stairway, and stooping, picked it up.

There was neither seal nor superscription upon the outside; therefore there seemed nothing wrong or dishonorable in opening it, for indeed how otherwise was she to learn to whom it belonged in order to restore it?

One glance told who was the writer (for she was no stranger to his peculiar chirography), to whom it was addressed, and what it signified.

"My Angel, one o'clock A. M. to-morrow. Signal, cry of an owl beneath your window. Carriage in waiting beyond the hedge.

"Your adorer."

That was all, but it needed not another word to let her, whose eyes now scanned it in indignant sorrow, fully into their plans.

She sent a quick glance around to satisfy herself that she was unseen, then crushing the missive in her hand, went on her way deeply thankful that Juliet had lost and that she had found it.

Yet she was sorely perplexed and anxious; so disturbed that it was no easy matter to give the necessary attention to her pupils. What should she do? Appeal again to Juliet? It seemed utterly useless. But this thing must be prevented; yes, even though it cost her the loss of her situation.

But, Harry! she shuddered and turned sick and faint at the thought that he might be taken, identified, and put on trial for the crime committed years ago. He must be saved at all risks. She would go out, meet and warn him ere he had quite reached Roselands.

He would be furious; perhaps in his rage do her some bodily harm; but—he must be saved.

She would give this note to Mr. Dinsmore, she decided, telling him where she had found it, that she had been well acquainted with the writer in former years, and recognized the hand.

That would be sufficient to lead him to prevent Juliet's leaving the house, and if she could succeed in warning Harry away, going and returning unobserved, all would be well.

But her plans miscarried. Mr. Dinsmore, as she learned on seeking an interview, had left home after an early breakfast, taken hastily in his private room, and would not probably return until the next day.

Here was an unexpected difficulty; what now was she to do?

She was slowly mounting the stairs in half despairing mood, when a pleasant, girlish voice addressed her from the hall below.

"Miss Worth, Pomp has just got back from the city with the mail, and here is a letter for you."

Mildred bounded up the stairs with the last words, put the letter into the eagerly outstretched hand of the governess, and hurried on to her own room to revel in the delights of a long epistle from her mother and sisters.

She was not half through it when there came a rap upon her door, and with brows knitting with vexation at the unwelcome interruption, she rose to open it.

She started back with an exclamation of surprise and terror as Miss Worth tottered in with a face white even to the lips, and sank speechless into the nearest chair.

"What is it? what is it?" cried Mildred hastening to bring a glass of water, and hold it to her lips.

The governess swallowed a mouthful, seemingly with some difficulty, then putting it aside with her hand, "Don't be alarmed," she whispered, " I shall be over it in a moment. But it was such a shock; oh, how could he—how could he be so wicked!"

She ended with a burst of weeping.

Mildred's sympathies were fully aroused; laying her precious letter carefully away for future perusal, she gave herself to the task of soothing and comforting the poor distracted woman.

Miss Worth told her story brokenly, still concealing the nature of the tie that connected her with the pseudo count.

Her letter, from her sister, Mrs. Marks, told of the return to America of their scapegrace brother, that he had paid them a flying visit weeks ago, and gone again, they knew not whither, and that shortly after his departure there had come to them a young, pretty Italian peasant woman, who claimed to be his wife; showing in proof thereof, some trinkets which they recognized as having belonged to him, a marriage certificate, and a baby boy, who was his image.

Miss Worth simply stated to Mildred the facts in regard to the note she had picked up and that her letter had brought certain intelligence that Juliet's admirer had already a living wife.

"Oh, dreadful!" cried Mildred, "now surely you will warn her once more?"

"Yes, I will; though doubtless she will refuse to believe it of him."

"But she will not, she cannot be so infatuated as to go on and elope with him without full proof that the story of his marriage is false."

"I do not know that: she is so supremely silly. But Miss Mildred, I must see her alone, and how am I to manage it? I have only to-day."

Mildred looked thoughtful. "I don't see how yet, but I must contrive to make an opportunity for you," she said; and after a little more talk about ways and means, mingled with some words of sympathy and hope from the younger to the older girl, they parted; Mildred going down to luncheon, Miss Worth to her own room.

Half an hour later Mildred joined her there with a face that told of good news before she opened her lips.

"Aunt Dinsmore thinks uncle may be home to-night," she said, " and I noticed Juliet did not seem pleased to hear it. She asked how soon, and aunt said probably not before half past one or two o'clock; as the train gets into the city about midnight and he must drive over from there.

"Then aunt proposed that we four ladies should take a drive this afternoon, and Reba and I accepted her invitation at once, but Juliet declined, saying she was tired and would find more enjoyment in a novel and the sofa."

"She stays at home to make her preparations," said Miss Worth.

"Just what I think; and this will be your opportunity," returned Mildred. " Is it not fortunate? Now I must go and leave you to improve it. The carriage will be at the door in a few moments."

Miss Worth sat down by her window to watch for it, and as soon as it had driven quite out of sight went quietly to Juliet's door and knocked.

There was no answer though she could hear some one moving softly about the room.

She waited a moment, then rapped again a little louder than before.

Still no notice was taken, the quiet footfalls

and slight rustle of silken garments continuing as before.

But she persisted, repeating her knocks at short intervals and with increasing force till at length the key was turned hastily in the lock and the door thrown open, showing Juliet's fair face crimson with passion.

"Will you cease that racket?" she began, then starting back at sight of the pale determined face, "*You!*" she cried, "is it *you?* How dare you?" and she would have slammed the door in the face of her unwelcome visitor, but Miss Worth was too quick for her, and holding it forcibly open, slipped in, pushed it to, turned the key, and facing the girl who stood spell-bound with astonishment and fury, said.

"I will not apologize for my seemingly rude behavior, since you have compelled me to it, and it is only for your own sake that I intrude upon you."

"Leave this room instantly!" was the passionate rejoinder, "instantly, do you hear?" stamping her foot with rage.

"Not till I have done my errand and cleared my skirts of your ruin, if you are still so infatuated as to rush upon it," returned the governess quietly, folding her arms and placing her back against the door.

"I have already told you the man who seeks your hand is a deceiver, a spurious nobleman, a mere fortune hunter—"

"Stop!" cried Juliet, interrupting her with fury in her tones and again stamping her foot, "stop! and leave this room or I will summon the servants to put you out."

"No, you will not do that," Miss Worth returned with a contemptuous smile, "you will not want them to hear what I have to tell of your adorer, or rather the adorer of your wealth —and I will not go till I have finished what I came to say."

"You think to rob me of him," sneered Juliet, "but you are mistaken. You are too old and ugly. If he ever fancied you it is all past; he can never do so again. But I can't believe you were ever really pretty, for you are as ugly as sin now."

"Thank you," the governess answered with irony. "I rejoice to learn that you think sin ugly, for it is a sin for you to allow this man to play the lover to you, and it would be a dreadful sin for you to marry him; not only because of the entire disapproval of your parents but," she added with strong emphasis, "because he *already has a wife.*"

For a moment Juliet was struck dumb with

astonishment, but recovering herself, "I don't believe it!" she cried, her cheek crimsoning, her eyes flashing. "I don't believe a word of it; and if I did I'd marry him all the same," she added, grinding her teeth. "I would, for I love him, I love him! and you needn't tell me he's a villain!"

"Marry him! the ceremony would be a mere farce, and you a—not a wife; for you could not be that while she lives who is his lawful, wedded wife."

Miss Worth spoke with slow distinctness, her eyes fixed severely upon Juliet's face.

The latter started back as if stung, then resuming her haughty, defiant air, "How dare you!" she repeated, "What is he to you? and what proof can you bring of all that you assert against him?"

"What he is to me does not concern you," said Miss Worth, "My knowledge of his marriage was gained to-day by a letter from his sister; but if I should show it to you, you would of course ask how you were to know that he was the man referred to, or that she was a reliable witness. No, I can prove nothing; but if you are wise you will require proof that he is—a man who has a right to offer you his hand;

who can make you his lawful wife; and whom to marry will not be ruin."

"Then I am not wise. Now go !"

"I obey you since my errand is now done," returned the governess with a stately bow, as she unlocked the door and threw it wide open.

Stepping into the hall she faced her antagonist again for an instant. "If you will persist in this madness, on your own head be your ruin; my skirts are clear," she said, and swept proudly away.

It cost Mildred quite an effort to give due attention to Reba's chatter and the small talk of her aunt, during the hour or more of their drive, her thoughts being very full of the interview then in progress between Miss Worth and Juliet.

On reaching home she repaired directly to the room of the former to hear an account of it.

This the governess gave in detail, concluding with, "You see, Miss Keith, it is just as I expected; she will not hear reason, she will take no warning, she is fully bent upon carrying out this mad freak, and if we save her, it will be in spite of herself."

"Yes; and we have but little time to consider how we shall do it," said Mildred. "What is your plan?"

" To go myself, a little before his appointed hour, to meet and warn him away, while you remain in the house and on the watch to prevent her from leaving it to join him. Are you willing to undertake that, Miss Mildred ? "

"Yes; to the best of my ability. I will rouse the whole house if necessary to prevent her from getting away with him."

" Thank you," Miss Worth said earnestly "Miss Keith, I am very sorry to have to call upon you for this assistance, for it will involve the loss of your night's rest. But Mr. Dinsmore being unfortunately away—"

" Don't speak of it," interrupted Mildred impulsively ; " it is a very small sacrifice on my part, for I am well and pretty strong again ; but you look wretchedly ill."

"Never mind me, I shall be better when this is over," Miss Worth answered with a faint smile.

" I will leave you to lie down and rest," Mildred said, rising to go ; " and can't you sleep through the early part of the night, if I am on guard and ready to wake you at midnight ? "

The governess shook her head. " I cannot sleep till this is over. But it will tend to lull Juliet's suspicions if you will retire at your asual early hour, and let me call you when the appointed hour draws near."

"It is a wise thought, and we will do so," Mildred said. "And now I must go and dress for dinner. Try not to be so very anxious. I do believe it will all turn out well," she added hopefully, as she left the room.

Chapter Sixteenth.

" Muse not that I thus suddenly proceed ;
For what I will, I will, and there's an end. '
—SHAKESPEARE.

THERE were guests from the neighborhood at both dinner and tea, some of whom remained during the evening.

Juliet was unusually gay and sprightly, but to Mildred, who watched her furtively, her unwonted mirthfulness seemed to cover other and deeper feelings. There were signs of agitation, perhaps unnoticed by a casual observer, a nervous tremor, a hectic flush on her cheek, a slight start at some sudden noise, or an unexpected address.

She was thrumming on the piano and shrieking out an air from a popular opera, at the top of her voice, when at ten o'clock, Mildred slipped quietly away to her own room.

Merely exchanging her evening dress for a neat dressing gown, Mildred threw herself upon a couch to await Miss Worth's summons, and contrary to her expectations, presently fell into a sound sleep.

She was awakened by a touch on the shoulder and started up to find the governess standing by her side.

"Will you come now?" she asked in low, agitated tones. "It is half past twelve, and I must start out at once."

"Yes, I am quite ready," Mildred answered, and wrapping a shawl about her shoulders, followed the lead of the governess.

A window on the landing of the principal staircase, down which Juliet would be likely to pass, was on the same side of the house with the one under which the signal was to be given.

There could be no better post of observation, and here Mildred seated herself, upon the broad sill, while her companion, parting from her with a whispered word of mingled thanks, caution and entreaty, glided down the stairs and let herself out at a side door, using extreme caution to make no noise.

Thence she gained the avenue, and beyond that the road. Here she paused and hesitated. She was not sure from which direction her brother would come: but she must make a choice

She did so and crept onward, keeping a narrow foot-path that ran parallel with the road, and between it and a hedge that enclosed the lawn and adjacent orchard.

Left thus alone, Mildred sat still, her heart beating fast with excitement and timidity, for the house was dark and silent almost as the grave.

But she bethought herself of Him to whom the night shineth as the day, and darkness and light are both alike, and with the thought grew calm and quiet. She was in the path of duty, and need fear no evil, because He was with her

Yet the waiting time seemed long. How would it end? If Miss Worth were successful, only in her stealthy return; otherwise probably with the signal and then a struggle between Juliet and herself.

She had begun to breathe more freely with the thought that the time for that must have passed, and was straining her ear to catch the faint sound of Miss Worth's approach, when the loud hoot of an owl from the shrubbery beneath the window, broke the silence with a suddenness that nearly startled her from her seat, and set her heart to throbbing wildly again.

She pressed her hand against her side to

still it, while she bent forward, listening intently for some answering sound from above.

A moment of utter stillness, then a slight creak, as of a door opened with extreme care, followed by other slight sounds as though some one were stealing softly down the hall, and Mildred slipped from her perch and back into the shadow of the wall, almost holding her breath for what was to come.

The stealthy step drew nearer; something was gliding past her when, with a quick movement, she stepped before, and threw her arms around it—a tall, slight figure muffled in a cloak.

There was a low, half stifled cry, then a struggle for release.

"Unhand me," muttered Juliet in a tone of intense, but suppressed fury. "Is there no limit to your insolent interference?"

"Juliet, it is I'" whispered Mildred, not relaxing her hold in the least. "I only want to save you from falling a prey to a villain who is after your money, would ruin you to get it: for he already has a wife."

"I don't believe a word of it! Let me go, let me go, I say!" and wrenching herself free she dealt Mildred a blow that sent her staggering against the wall.

But she recovered herself instantly and sprang after Juliet, who was gliding down the stairs toward the lower hall.

She caught her as they reached the hall below.

"Juliet, Juliet, are you mad?" she panted; "will you forsake all you love—all that life holds dear for that scoundrel?"

"What business is it of yours?" demanded Juliet fiercely, and trying with all her strength to shake her off. "I tell you I will not be prevented by you or anybody. Let go of me, I say, or I will do you a mischief."

"I will not let you go," returned Mildred. "Come back or I will call aloud and rouse the house." What would have happened it is impossible to tell, had not help come at that precise moment.

A carriage had driven up to the front entrance, the rumble of its wheels sending the cowardly villain in the shrubbery flying to the adjacent woods.

The girls, in the excitement of their struggle, had not heard its approach, but the sudden opening of the front door, and the sound of **Mr.** Dinsmore's step and voice as he entered, accompanied by his body servant, to whom he was giving some order as to the disposal of his luggage, caused them to loose their hold of each other.

Juliet darted up the stairs, while Mildred dropped into a chair; her strength completely forsaking her with the withdrawal of the necessity for its exertion.

" Who is here ? " demanded Mr. Dinsmore, his ear catching the rustle of Juliet's garments and the sound of Mildred's heavy breathing.

" Solon, strike a light instantly."

" It is I, uncle," panted Mildred, bursting into hysterical sobs.

" You, Mildred ! " he exclaimed in utter astonishment as he recognized the voice. " Why, child, what on earth are you doing here at this time of night ?   All in the dark too. What has gone wrong ? are you sick ? "

Solon had struck a match and succeeded in lighting the hall lamp, and with Mr. Dinsmore's last question its rays fell full upon Mildred's face, showing it pale, agitated, and with eyes brimming with tears.

" Why, you are as white as a sheet ! " he exclaimed, laying his hand affectionately on her shoulder.   " Child, child, what is the matter ? "

In a few rapid, rather incoherent sentences, she gave him an inkling of the state of affairs ; to which he returned a volley of questions, and without waiting for an answer to any of them "Out into the shrubbery, Solon," he commanded, "call Ajax and Pomp, to help ; catch the rascal if you can, and bring him to me."

Then to Mildred, repeating his queries, "Where is Juliet!" he asked. "Where is Miss Worth? How does she come to know about the villain or his plot to carry off Juliet? what is he to her?"

"I don't know, sir, what he is to her," said Mildred, "but she says she has known him all his life, and a letter she received to-day told her of his marriage ; that he has a living wife."

"He has? the scoundrel!" cried her listener.

"Yes sir ; and of course, on learning that, Miss Worth was more than ever determined to frustrate his plans."

"Well, what more, and where is this precious fool of a Juliet? I wish all girls were blessed with your common sense, child."

"She ran up stairs as you came in, sir."

"And may have come down by the back stairway and made off with the rascal, after all!" he exclaimed in alarm. "Run up to her room, Milly, and see if she is there, while I look about below here."

Mildred went at once, though she would much rather have been excused; for the errand was no pleasant one; she was very reluctant to meet Juliet again at that moment; but fortunately was spared the necessity, as, on nearing the door of Juliet's sleeping room, she distinctly heard her voice in conversation with Reba.

She hurried down again with her report, which her uncle received with grim satisfaction.

"That is well," he said. "Now I'll join in the search for the scoundrel, and I promise you that if we catch him, he'll not get away unhurt. But where is Miss Worth, child? you have not answered that question yet."

As he spoke, a side door opened, and a tall black robed figure glided in.

"Miss Worth!" he exclaimed, catching sight of her face.

"Yes," she said in a hoarse whisper, leaning back against the wall, and looking ready to faint.

"You are ill," he said; "let me help you into the library and give you a glass of wine."

She hardly seemed to hear him. Her eyes were fixed in eager, terrified questioning upon Mildred's face.

"Juliet is in her room," the latter hastened to say.

"'Thank God for that!" she said in quivering tones. "And he?"

"Is gone, I suppose. No one has seen him, as far as I know."

At that moment one of the men put his head in at the door. "Can't find the rascal, massa; reckon he dun gone cl'ar off de place."

"Quite likely; but as he may return, you are to be on the watch till sunrise," was the reply.

"You didn't meet him?" Mildred asked, drawing near the governess, and speaking in an undertone.

"No; I must have taken the wrong road. Mr. Dinsmore, I owe you an explanation. Shall it be given now?"

The voice was very low, very tremulous, but the sad eyes were lifted unflinchingly to his stern face.

"As you please," he said, his features softening a little at sight of her distress. "You look hardly able to make it now, and some hours later will answer just as well. Indeed, I think we would all do well to go to our beds as soon as possible. But stay a moment."

He stepped into the dining-room, and returned with a glass of wine, which he offered to the governess, saying, "You look ready to faint; drink this, it will do you good."

"No, no, never!" she cried, shuddering and recoiling as from a serpent; "it has been the ruin of those I love best."

"Very well," he said coldly, "Mildred, will you take it?"

"No, thank you, uncle; I do not need it and would rather not," the young girl answered pleasantly.

"Silly girl," he said, draining the glass himself. "Well, good night, ladies; or rather good morning. Miss Worth, I will see you in the library directly after breakfast."

So saying he left them.

"What a blessing that it has turned out so well," Mildred said to her companion.

"Has it?" queried the governess, in a bewildered tone, and putting her hand to her head. "I feel as though the earth were reeling beneath my feet. I can not think."

"Let me help you to your room; a few hours' rest will make all right again with you, I trust," Mildred said compassionately.

"Don't allow yourself to feel anxious or distressed," she went on, as she assisted her up the stairs. "I am sure uncle will not be hard with you when he learns how free from blame you are; Juliet has been saved, and he seems to have escaped, and will not be likely to try it again."

" Ah, if I could have met and warned him, sighed the governess.

" Surely it is better as it is, since he has got away without," reasoned Mildred: " for might he not have been angry and abusive ? "

" True, too true ! " she murmured, catching at the balusters to keep from falling ; " yes, it is better so ; but my brain reels and I cannot think."

Mildred was alarmed. " What can I do for you ? " she asked.

" Nothing, nothing, but help me to my bed, thank you, I shall be better when I have slept off this horrible fatigue and weakness. Oh, such a tramp and weary waiting as it was !—out in the cold and darkness on a lonely road," she gasped shudderingly, as she sank down upon her bed. " It seemed as if I should drop down and die before I could get back to the house. And my terror for him ! that was the worst of all ! "

" I don't think he deserves your love and care for him ! " Mildred said, her indignation waxing hot against the worthless villain.

" Perhaps not," she sighed, " but he loved me once, and he was a noble fellow then. And I—ah, he told me I had helped to ruin him ! "

" But it wasn't true ? " Mildred said in a tone of indignant inquiry.

Miss Worth did not seem to hear. " I shall

do now," she said presently, "and you need rest. Do go to your bed, Miss Mildred. Perhaps I shall sleep if left alone."

Perceiving that she could be of no further assistance, Mildred went not unwillingly, for she too was quite worn out with fatigue and excitement.

It was eight o'clock when she woke, but she was ready for the summons to breakfast, which was not served that morning until near nine.

Juliet did not make an appearance at the meal. She was indisposed, Reba reported, and would take a cup of tea in her own room.

"The best place for her," commented Mr. Dinsmore shortly.

"What do you mean by that?" queried his wife, who had heard nothing of the occurrences of the past night.

"Just what I say and I hope she will have the grace to stay there till her father comes for her, as I requested him to do by this morning's mail."

"Mr. Dinsmore, *will* you explain yourself?" exclaimed his wife in a tone of exasperation.

"It will not require many words," he answered drily. "She would have eloped with another woman's husband last night if she had not been hindered."

"Another woman's husband!" echoed Reba in astonishment and dismay—"I did not know it was so bad as that!"

"Dreadful! impossible!" cried Mrs. Dinsmore, dropping her knife and fork and bursting into tears. "Don't tell me a niece of mine could do such a thing as that! Mr. Dinsmore, it's a cruel joke."

"No joke at all," he said, "but the simple, unvarnished truth; though of course she refused to believe that the man was married."

"And who is the wretch?" cried his wife, grinding her teeth. "If you'd been half a man, you'd have shot him down!"

"I'm no murderer, madam," was the biting retort, "and in my opinion a cowhiding would much better befit so cowardly a scoundrel. I should have administered that with hearty good will, could I have laid hands on him."

"I wish you had!" she exclaimed with passionate vehemence. "I am glad you wrote for Mr. Marsden, and I hope he will come at once and take that shameful girl away before she does anything more to bring disgrace on the family. Reba, why did you let her do so?"

"I, Aunt Belle? I'm not in her confidence, and was as ignorant and innocent as yourself in regard to the whole thing."

"Who did hinder her? am I not to hear the whole story?" demanded Mrs. Dinsmore, turning to her spouse again.

"I presume it will all be unfolded to you in time," was the cool reply. "I have not heard it fully myself yet. Mildred here," and he looked pleasantly at her, "knows more about it than I do; and to her, I believe, our thanks are due for preventing the mischief."

"To Miss Worth, uncle, much more than to me," Mildred said, blushing and feeling decidedly uncomfortable under the surprised, scrutinizing glances of her aunt and Reba. "It was she who found it all out, tried to persuade Juliet to give it up, and when she failed in that, told me—"

"Told you!" interrupted Mrs. Dinsmore, with indignation. "Why did she not come to me instead? I was the proper person by all odds."

Mildred was at a loss for a reply that should not damage the cause of the governess; but Mr. Dinsmore came to her relief. "I presume, my dear, it was to save you from the mortification of hearing of your niece's contemplated folly, and her from that of having you made acquainted with it."

Chapter Seventeenth.

Do not insult calamity :
It is a barbarous grossness to lay on
The weight of scorn, when heavy misery
Too much already weighs men's fortunes down."

—Daniel.

RETURNING to her room to don her riding habit, directly after breakfast, Mildred met Miss Worth on her way to the library to keep her appointment with Mr. Dinsmore.

"How pale and ill you look!" exclaimed Mildred.

"Ah, you would not wonder if you knew how I shrink from this interview," sighed the governess.

"I think you need not," Mildred answered kindly; then gave her the substance of the conversation at the table, in regard to the past night's occurrences, adding that her uncle's explanation of her probable motives had entirely appeased Mrs. Dinsmore's anger, and presumably he did not himself hold her in great disfavor.

"How very good in you to tell me, Miss Keith," the governess said, grateful tears springing to her eyes. "But I must not delay another moment, lest I keep him waiting."

She hastened on into the library, and was relieved to find it tenantless. Unpunctuality would not have helped her cause, and though the moments of waiting tried her already over-strained nerves, she was thankful that they had fallen to her lot rather than to his.

She had slept little, waking early, not greatly refreshed, and tormented with anxiety in regard to her brother's whereabouts, likelihood to renew his attempt to carry off Juliet, and danger of arrest on the old charges. This in addition to the care that came upon her every day :—the ever recurring question how she was to meet necessary expenses for herself and those dependent upon her.

Almost too weary to stand, yet too restless to remain quiet, she dropped into a chair for a moment, then rose and paced the floor, at last pausing beside the fire, and standing there with her right elbow on the mantel, her forehead in the open palm of her hand, her eyes cast down, while painful thought surged through her brain.

Thus Mr. Dinsmore found her, so absorbed in her meditations that she was not aware of his entrance until he coughed slightly to attract her attention. Then she came out of her reverie with a start.

"Excuse me, sir, but I was not aware that I was no longer alone."

"Time enough," he said; "and let me compliment you on being more punctual than myself. But you are not looking well or happy."

"No, sir; and I think you will hardly wonder that I do not, when you have heard what I am here to tell."

"Be seated," he said, waving his hand toward an easy chair, while taking possession of its fellow, "and let me hear what it is."

She seemed at a loss where to begin her story, and to help her he remarked interrogatively, "I presume you have no objection to explaining the cause of your mysterious nocturnal ramble?"

"No," she said, "I went to warn that man away from the house."

"Ah! yes, that may have been the better plan, as I was absent from home; but what puzzles me is to understand how you knew of his coming."

"I had picked this up in the hall," she said, handing him the little note.

"But how could it tell you so much, since

it gives neither the name of the writer nor that of the person addressed ? "

" The man's writing is perfectly familiar to me," she explained, growing a shade paler as she spoke; " I have known him intimately for years, and had learned from him his designs upon Miss Marsden."

" An intimate acquaintance of yours ! " he exclaimed in astonishment. " Not one to be proud of, certainly. May I ask a further expla- nation ? It is a matter of some consequence to know with what style of persons the instructress of my children associates."

"I know it; you have a perfect right to ask," she stammered, a crimson blush suffusing her cheek, hot tears rushing into the downcast eyes. "Oh, may you never know, Mr. Dins- more, what it is to have those nearest and dear- est bring shame and disgrace upon you ! "

" A relative ? " he asked. " Is he not a foreigner ? "

She shook her head sorrowfully, and after a moment's struggle for composure, told him what the man was to her, how he had been led astray by love for the wine-cup, and the evil influence of an older villain ; that he had left his country years ago, traveling his family knew not whither, and how unexpectedly she had re-

cognized him in the pseudo Count of whom
Juliet had become enamored; how she had
entreated him to go away, and failing to persuade him, had made a fruitless appeal to
Juliet, disclosing his real character and aims;
but only to be scouted at and contemned as an
envious rival; then had sought for him with
the purpose of calling in his aid to save the
wilful girl from the destruction she courted,
and failing to find him had enlisted Mildred in
the cause.

"Miss Marsden is a born simpleton!" he
commented impatiently. "Well, Miss Worth,
she owes a great deal to your good sense and
right feeling. I, too, am obliged to you. I
sympathize with you in the trial of having such
a brother, and do not see that you have been
at all to blame in this unfortunate matter; but
rather the contrary.

"However, Mrs. Dinsmore is not always entirely reasonable in her views and require-
ments, and it is altogether likely would object
longer receiving your services as governess to
her children, if she knew of your relationship
to this man. We will, therefore, keep that
matter to ourselves."

So saying, he dismissed her and the subject together, with a wave of his hand; and

she withdrew with one burden somewhat lightened.

For some days nothing special occurred at Roselands; Juliet kept to her own apartments; for the most part alone, or with no companionship but that of her maid ; for Reba's strongly expressed disgust and indignation at her folly had sent her into a fit of the pouts, so that they had small relish for each other's society ; and Mrs. Dinsmore, angry with her for the disgrace she had so nearly brought upon the family, would not go near her, nor allow any of the children to do so.

Mildred, too, stayed away, partly in obedience to a hint from her aunt, and partly because she did not suppose her company would be acceptable ; she and Juliet having never been kindred spirits.

Meanwhile, Miss Worth still took her meals in the nursery with the younger children, doing so of choice, attended faithfully to her duties in the schoolroom, but was seldom seen at other times.   Her light often burned far into the night, and day by day she grew thinner and paler her cheeks more sunken, her eyes more hollow, her step slower and more languid.

Mildred alone seemed to note the change, but to her kind inquiries the governess always answered that she was well, and that in a tone that did not encourage further inquiry or remark.

Mr. Marsden was slow in responding to Mr. Dinsmore's summons, but at length a letter was received, announcing his intention of starting on his journey two days after date, and requesting Mr. Dinsmore to keep a vigilant watch over Juliet until his arrival.

It had come by the mail, which, arriving in the city the previous night, was brought to Roselands by Pomp, in the morning.

Mr. Dinsmore opened it at the breakfast table, read it to himself, and with a satisfied smile, passed it on to his wife for her perusal, while he opened the newspaper, and leisurely glanced over its contents.

"Ah!" he exclaimed presently, with some excitement, "here is a bit of news.   Listen!"

He read it aloud.

"Yesterday, a gentleman from Philadelphia, visiting in our city, met in the street, and recognized an old acquaintance, one Henry Worth, formerly of Philadelphia, who, some five years ago, fled thence to escape trial on a charge of forgery. Worth was of respectabl: family; his father had been a man of very considerable wealth, but had failed shortly before the commission of the crime; brought to ruin, it is said, by the excesses of this son.

"The young man has been leading a gay life of late, in the assumed character of a French nobleman—calling himself the Count DeLisle The gentleman above referred to promptly reported his case to the police; he was arrested and is now safely lodged in prison; whence he will be sent north in a few days for trial."

"So it's all true—that he was a scoundrel!" cried Mrs. Dinsmore, "and his name's Worth! He's Miss Worth's brother! I know it! I'm sure of it! and that accounts for her knowing all about him. The wicked, deceitful thing to hide it as she has done, and impose herself— the sister of a convict—on me as governess to my children! I never heard of anything so shameful! I'll give her notice at once, and—"

"Why, my dear, what absurd folly!" exclaimed Mr. Dinsmore impatiently, angry with her for her unreasonable displeasure, and with himself for having inadvertently read out the name; "what difference does it make?"

"What difference, Mr. Dinsmore! are you crazy? You may consider paupers and convicts proper associates for your children, but they are not for mine, and that woman shall go."

"She is neither a pauper nor a convict," he

said, " nor in the least responsible, so far as I have been able to learn, for the wrong doing of this man, whom, by the way, you do not know to be her brother; and if he is, I should think a woman's heart would feel for her in the terrible sorrow and disgrace of having such a relative."

" Papa, what is a convict ? " asked Lora.

" One legally proved guilty of a crime," he said; " and, my dear, the term does not yet apply to the man himself, (much less to your governess) as he has not yet been brought to trial."

" It s all the same," she sneered, " for I haven't a doubt of his guilt. There, you needn't smile, as if I had said a foolish thing ! "

" I wish you would not *do* a foolish thing in sending away one so well qualified for her duties, and faithful in their performance, as Miss Worth, merely because she is so unfortunate as to bear the same name—possibly be nearly related to—a scamp."

" Dear me, papa, I think mamma is quite right," remarked Louise, with a toss of her head. " I'm sure I don't wish to be taught by such a person."

" When your opinion is desired, Louise, it will oe called for," said her father severely. " In the meantime you may reserve it."

"Well, I mean to ask Miss Worth if that man is her brother?" muttered the child sullenly.

"You will do no such thing!" returned her father. "I will not have a word said to her about it."

At that his wife smiled significantly.

"It might be as well to show that paragraph to Juliet," she said, rising from the table. "Suppose you give me the paper."

"Do so, by all means," he replied, handing it to her.

"Mildred, here is something for Miss Worth. Will you see that she gets it?"

It, too, was a newspaper, and Mildred hoped compassionately, as she carried it up stairs, that it did not contain the item of distressing news for Miss Worth that her uncle had read from the other.

Mrs. Dinsmore had preceded her by several minutes, and her voice speaking in cold, cutting tones, came to the girl's ear, from the upper hall, as she set her foot upon the first stair.

"You must be aware that your services are no longer acceptable here," she was saying "In fact you would never have been given the situation had I known of this disgraceful con nection; and I must say I am justly indignant at the gross deception that has been practiced upon me."

"She must be speaking to Miss Worth; oh, what cruel words!" thought Mildred.

She had reached the landing, and turning to ascend the short flight above, caught sight of the speaker and the person addressed.

Miss Worth stood leaning against the wall, one hand clutching at the balustrade for support, her face deathly pale, and her lips trembling; Mrs. Dinsmore standing a few feet from her, gathering her dainty skirts close to her person as if fearful of contamination, her aristocratic nose high in the air, her countenance expressing scorn, contempt, and righteous indignation.

"What have you to say for yourself?" she demanded.

"Nothing, but that I am guiltless of any intentional wrong," the governess replied, lifting her head, and speaking in a tone of quiet despair, "and that I have faithfully performed my duties to the best of my ability."

"You don't deny, then, that this scoundrel. this felon—"

"Madame," interrupted the governess, her eyes flashing, while a bright red spot burned on each cheek, "he is not that, for he has never been convicted of, nor so much as brought to trial for any crime."

"Insolence!" exclaimed Mrs. Dinsmore. 'Well, if he hasn't been yet, he soon will be, and get his deserts, I sincerely hope."

And picking up the newspaper, which seemed to have dropped from Miss Worth's nerveless hand, she swept on toward Juliet's apartments; in another moment had disappeared within them, shutting the door after her.

The fire had died out of Miss Worth's eye, the red had left her cheek, and she was swaying from side to side; only her hold on the balustrade keeping her from falling.

Mildred sprang toward her. "Lean on me," she said. "Let me help you to your room. Don't be so troubled; the Lord will take care of you and yours, if you put your trust in Him."

She did not know whether or not her words were heard and understood. The poor woman answered only with a heavy sigh and whispered, "Thank you. I shall be better soon. But oh, what will become of them all! my mother, my poor mother! He was her pride, her idol!"

Sympathetic tears streamed over Mildred's cheeks as she assisted her to her room.

" I'm to go away, Miss Mildred," she said,
" turned off in disgrace for what is no fault of
mine: no fault but my bitter, bitter sorrow!
God help me and those dependent on me!"

" He will," Mildred answered chokingly;
" He is so kind, so full of compassion; His tender mercies are over all his works!"

She stayed a little while trying to adminis-
ter consolation, then putting the paper into
Miss Worth's hands, merely saying that it had
come by that morning's mail, she went away.

Finding Rachel busy in her room, she
stepped back into the hall and stood for a few
moments at the window there, looking out into
the avenue below where Mr. Dinsmore was
mounting his horse to make his daily morning
round of the plantation.

Suddenly there was a sound in Miss Worth's
room as of a heavy body falling to the floor.

Mildred ran to her door, and rushing in
without the ceremony of knocking, found the
poor governess stretched, apparently lifeless,
upon the floor, the newspaper lying by her
side.

Mildred's eye, as she stooped over the pros-
trate form, was caught by a paragraph that was
heavily marked.

But the present was no time to examine it,

and pushing the paper aside, she hastened to loosen the clothing of the fainting woman, at the same time giving directions to the two or three servants who had been attracted by the noise of the fall, and followed her into the room.

"Throw up that window, Minerva! Some cold water, Fanny, quick, quick! And you, Rachel, run to my room for my smelling salts."

' O, Miss Milly, is she done gone dead?" asked Fanny fearfully, as she sprinkled the water upon the still, white face.

"No, no; it's only a bad faint," Mildred answered, but her own heart quaked with fear as she spoke; the pinched features were so deathlike in their fixedness and palloi.

And spite of every effort they remained so till, nearly wild with terror, Mildred bade the servants summon other assistance.

"Call Mrs. Brown," she said. "Ask aunt if we shall not send for the doctor."

They hurried away to do her bidding, while she renewed her exertions, sending up silent, importunate petitions the while to her heavenly Friend.

They were answered; Miss Worth sighed deeply, opened her eyes and lifted them to the young face bent over her, with a look of such hopeless, heart-breaking anguish, that the girl burst into sobs and tears.

"Oh, what is it? what is it?" she said.

"He—he was my husband—and—and I *loved him*," came in a hoarse whisper from the colorless lips, and with the last word she swooned again.

"She has lost her reason," thought Mildred. "Poor, poor thing! oh, perhaps it may be better for her if she never comes to herself again."

Chapter Eighteenth.

"Never morning wore
To evening, but some heart did break."
—TENNYSON.

THEY brought the housekeeper and the family physician. The latter pronounced the patient very ill, and with good reason; for she passed out of one swoon only to fall into another, till they thought that her end was surely near at hand.

However after some hours the immediate danger seemed over and the doctor left, promising to return before night.

Mrs. Dinsmore had been awed and frightened into something slightly akin to terror and remorse on account of her excessive harshness, but now shook it off.

"Really she takes her dismissal very hard," she remarked to Mildred as the latter was leaving the dinner table. "I had no idea she was so much attached to Roselands."

"I do not think it could be that alone, aunt," Mildred returned in surprise and disgust.

"What then ? "

"Her relative's disgrace ; the poverty and distress to herself and a mother and sister dependent on her, consequent on being thrown out of employment."

Then with a sudden recollection of that paper with its marked paragraph, Mildred hastened from the room and went in search of it.

The patient had fallen asleep, Rachel watching at her side.

A glance showed Mildred the paper folded and laid upon the table. She opened it cautiously, found the article she sought and read it.

"A case of lynching occurred in one of the southern counties of Texas, about two weeks ago. A man named Joseph White, said to be from one of the Northern States, suspected of horse stealing, was taken by a posse of some forty armed men, carried into the woods and hung. He was given ten minutes to prepare for death ; died bravely, protesting his innocence to the last ; but of course nobody believed him, as the proof against him was strong."

Sick and faint with horror, Mildred laid down the paper and dropped, shuddering, into

a chair. Oh, this was worse than all! If he
was that poor woman's husband, and she loved
him, no wonder news so dreadful, and coming
at such a time as this, should bring her down
to the very gates of death.

The girlish heart was filled with a great
compassion for the poor stricken creature, a
great longing to comfort her in her grief and
desolation.

"She will not live, she cannot," she whispered to herself; "I should not wish to were I
in her place; for oh, it is so horrible, so horrible! How can men be such savages as to take
human life to atone for the loss of an animal!
and that perhaps the life of an innocent man?"

"I should be loath to assume your responsibility in this matter," remarked Mr. Dinsmore to his wife, as Mildred left them lingering
over their dessert.

"Why?" she demanded, bridling; "did *I*
cause the ruin of her brother or the poverty of
the family?"

"You seem to have added to that last burden; thus supplying the one drop that makes
the cup overflow."

"I only did my duty to my children," she
retorted angrily.

"I cannot see it," he said; "the children

have improved very much in the two years that she has been with us."

"And of course all the credit of that belongs to her! there is none at all due to me. I often wonder, Mr. Dinsmore, how you came to marry a woman for whom you entertain so little admiration or respect."

"That is hardly a fair inference from what I have said," he rejoined in a tone of weariness and disgust; for she had tried his patience not a little that day with her whims and follies.

He rose with the last word and withdrew to the library. He was sitting before the fire in his easy chair, seemingly lost in thought, when the door opened softly and Mildred glided across the room and stood at his side.

As he looked up he saw that her features were working with emotion, her eyes full of tears.

"What is it?" he asked, in a startled tone; "she's not gone, I hope?"

Mildred shook her head, and with a burst of tears and a whispered "I could almost wish she was if—if I was quite sure she was prepared," pointed significantly to the marked paragraph in the paper which she held before him.

He read it, and then looked up at her with an inquiring "Well?" upon which Mildred told her reasons for connecting that item of news with Miss Worth's sudden seizure, repeating the words gasped out by the pale, trembling lips of the governess on her partial restoration to consciousness.

"I thought then that her mind wandered," concluded Mildred, "but since reading this, I fear her words were only too true."

"Poor thing!" he sighed. "I'm afraid she knows by sad experience all that she rescued Juliet from. Well, Milly, we will do the best we can for her. And, child, don't distress yourself unnecessarily. It will do her no good, you know."

"You are always kind and thoughtful for me, uncle," she responded gratefully, "but this seems no time to be considering myself. Do you know what the doctor thinks of her?"

"He told me that the attack must have been occasioned by some severe mental shock coming upon an exhausted frame. What she has had to exhaust her I don't know—her duties were light enough, I supposed—but the shock I took to have been the arrest of her brother. It would seem, however, from this, that a far more terrible one was superadded."

"Yes," Mildred said, shuddering. "Oh, my heart bleeds for her. But how strange that she is married Why should she have kept it so profound a secret? going back to her maiden name?"

"That I cannot tell," Mr. Dinsmore answered; "but probably it was a clandestine and unfortunate affair, and she wished to avoid unpleasant explanations. We will say nothing about it to your aunt, as it would only increase her displeasure against the unhappy woman?"

"Ah, uncle," Mildred said musingly, "how little idea I have had hitherto of the dreadful distress that comes into some lives! I begin to think myself a very fortunate mortal."

"It is well to learn to appreciate our blessings," he returned with a smile that had little of mirth in it; for he was thinking with concern of the condition and prospects of the stranger within his gates.

"I must ask Dr. Barton whether she is likely to be long ill," he said, thinking aloud rather than addressing Mildred, "that we may make arrangements accordingly. And I think we should show him this," indicating the fatal news item.

"It is her secret," Mildred suggested doubtfully

"True, my dear, but physicians have often to be entrusted with the secrets of their patients, and Dr. Barton is a safe depository for such things."

Mrs. Dinsmore was impatient for Dr. Barton's opinion, very impatient over the unfortunate circumstances of the serious seizure of the governess underneath her roof; for she entertained an utter detestation of sickness and death, and was always ready to fly from them at a moment's warning; whatever might be the character of the illness, she insisted there was danger of contagion, and saw it to be clearly her duty to take care of herself by running away.

She spent the afternoon in overseeing the packing of trunks, that she might be prepared for any emergency; then anxiously awaited the doctor's report.

It was her husband who brought it to her at last, late in the evening. He had been closeted for a quarter of an hour with the physician, and now came into his wife's boudoir with a countenance full of grave concern.

" Well, what is it? what does Dr. Barton say?" she queried fretfully, " I thought you would never come back to tell me."

" He fears there is little hope of recovery." her husband answered gravely, pacing slowly to and fro with the air of one who is seriously disturbed.

" Ana is she going to be sick long ? "

" It may be for some weeks, he cannot tell certainly."

" Can she be moved ? "

" Moved ? What occasion for that ? The room she occupies now is comfortable ; is it not?"

" Dear me, Mr. Dinsmore, you can be very stupid ! I want to know if she can't be sent to the village to a hotel or boarding house. It isn't at all pleasant to think of her dying here. I don't want any haunted rooms in my house."

He paused in his walk, and stood looking at her in amazement, that presently gave place to an expression of extreme chagrin and disgust.

" Isabella ! " he exclaimed, " are you utterly heartless ? utterly destitute of womanly compassion for the helpless and suffering ? "

" Of course I'm not," she said, resorting to tears, as was her wont when at a loss for better weapons of defence. " I'm sure she could be made very comfortable there, and I spared the necessity of being turned out of my own home in the depth of winter. But you can think of everybody's comfort and happiness except your wife's ; *it* isn't of the least consequence, and never will be."

" Really," he said, " I do not know what

you are talking about. I certainly have not proposed your leaving home, and cannot see the slightest necessity for your doing so."

"No, you would be quite as well pleased to have me stay here and get sick and die, and give you a chance to find a younger and prettier wife."

He disdained a reply to that, and presently she went on :

"I shall take the children, and go to Kentucky to visit my sister. It's fortunate that Mr. Marsden comes to-morrow, and is going to return immediately. I could not have a better escort."

"As you please ; I have become somewhat used to being left out of my wife's plans," he said coldly, turning on his heel to leave the room. "Go if you like," he added, turning toward her again, " but don't talk of necessity ; for there is not the remotest danger of Miss Worth's sickness proving contagious. She is dying of a broken heart."

"Ridiculous !" she muttered as he went out and shut the door, " the idea of a governess coming to such a romantic end . It's far more likely to turn out scarlet fever or small-pox."

By morning she had worked herself up to the belief that such was really the case.

The next step was to bring her nieces to a like conviction ; in which she succeeded so well that they were greatly alarmed, Juliet nearly forgetting the disappointment and disgrace of her late attempt at elopement, in the fear that small-pox might rob her of her beauty.

She had not much to lose, to be sure, but of that fact she was comfortably ignorant, and as what she had was but skin deep, small, pox would have made sad havoc with it.

Mr. Marsden arrived in the evening, and early the following morning the whole party, consisting of himself and his two daughters, Mrs. Dinsmore and her six children, with their nurses, set out for his home in Kentucky.

They departed without seeing Mildred, who had been so much in the sick-room that they were afraid of her, but left good-bye for her with Mr. Dinsmore.

He made no effort to detain his family, but simply remarked to his wife, on taking leave of her, that when she felt it safe to return, he would be happy to see her and their children.

The house seemed strangely quiet and deserted as he turned back into it after seeing them off.

He went up to the sick-room. Mildred was

there, moving softly about, supplementing the work of the housemaid with a few skillful touches here and there, that seemed to brighten up the place wonderfully.

He had said to her at the first, " Mildred, you are not to bear any part of this burden. Mrs. Brown and Aunt Delia are both excellent nurses, and will not neglect anything that can be done for her relief or restoration ; and I cannot have you wearing yourself out."

He said substantially the same thing now, speaking in an undertone that could not disturb the patient, who was sleeping under the influence of medicine.

" I shall not wear myself out, uncle, never fear," she answered in the same low key, smiling up affectionately into his face, " but I cannot be content to stay away all the time, for she seems to cling to me."

" Yes," said Mrs. Brown, coming in ; " and Miss Mildred has a wonderfully soothing way with her that quiets her in her fits of restlessness and distress, when nothing else can.

" And I think, Mr. Dinsmore," she added, in a still lower tone, " that it won't be long the poor creature will be troubling any of us. I see death in her pale, sunken face now."

Mildred stole out into the hall, and her uncle

following her, found her wiping away the fast-falling tears.

" O, uncle," she sobbed, " what do you think I have discovered ? that she has been wearing herself out sitting up half the night, for months past, writing articles and stories for newspapers and magazines, in order to earn a little more for the support of that mother and sister."

"Indeed!" he said, looking much concerned. "I am very sorry; I would rather have added a hundred dollars to her salery, if I had known it. But unfortunately it is too late now."

"I can't help feeling angry at them!" cried Mildred; "why didn't they bear their own burdens according to the Bible command? And then that brother—and husband! Oh, it is too bad!"

" Have you learned any more of her story?" he asked.

"No, sir; she hardly speaks at all except that I have heard her murmur to herself in, oh, such a heart broken way, ' My darling, my darling, oh, my darling?' and two or three times she has whispered to me, ' Tell me about Him-- that Friend.' "

"That Friend? whom does she mean?"

" The Lord Jesus   I told her of Him once

when 1 found her sad and troubled, and it seemed to do her good."

"You are a blessed little comforter! you must have taken lessons of your mother," he said in a moved tone, as he turned and went away.

Going down stairs, he ordered his carriage and drove over to Ion.

When he returned, Mrs. Travilla was with him.

It was a glad surprise to Mildred, a greater comfort than anything else but the arrival of her own mother could have been; for here was one with a heart ever tenderly alive to human woe, and far more capable than herself of pointing the sufferer to the only true source of help and consolation.

Together they watched, day after day, by the sick and dying bed; for the poor woman had indeed received her death blow in that last terrible announcement.

She said little, made no complaint, but lay there growing weaker, and often lifting her eyes to their faces with a look of hopeless anguish in them that wrung their hearts.

Then Mrs. Travilla would lean over her and in low, tender tones tell of the love and sympathy of Jesus, repeating now one, now another

of the many exceeding great and precious promises of His word.

"'As one whom his mother comforteth so
will I comfort you; and ye shall be com
forted.'

"'Come unto me, all ye that labor and are
heavy laden, and I will give you rest.'

"'I have loved them with an everlasting
love.'

"'I will never leave thee nor forsake thee.'"

"Ah, if He loves me, why does He send
such fearful trials?" she asked one day.

"My dear," said Mrs. Travilla, "He told his
disciples, 'In the world ye shall have tribulation; but be of good cheer, I have overcome
the world.'

"'We must through much tribulation enter
into the kingdom of God.' But 'our light
affliction, which is but for a moment, worketh
for us a far more exceeding and eternal weight
of glory.'

"Trust Him and He will do for you just
what is best; will give you strength to bear all
that He sends, and take you at last to Himself
to be unspeakably happy forever and forever."

"I will, I do," she said. "Ah, Miss Keith,"
turning her sad eyes upon Mildred, who sat
near with tears streaming down her cheeks, "I

thank God that you were sent here to tell me of this heavenly Friend! for His love is all that sustains me in this dread hour."

She closed her eyes, and for some moments they thought she slept; but opening them again, "I am dying," she whispered; "but I am not afraid, for He is with me. Ah, how much easier than *his* death—*his*—*my darling's!* she added with a shudder. "Only ten minutes to prepare; and—I—fear he had never found this Friend."

The keenest look of anguish they had ever seen came into her eyes with those words, and for some minutes she was too much overcome to proceed.

When at last she did it was in tones so low and tremulous that they strained their ears to catch the sounds.

"Six years ago we married; secretly,—against my parents' wishes. They were right; he was wild—loved wine, cards, fast horses, but me too, and oh, *how* I loved him! He was Harry's ruin; both had to fly, and I have never taken his name openly; no one knew what he was to me, but my own family; and I thought no one need know. Perhaps it was wrong—but how could I bare my heart to a stranger?"

"You were not called upon to do so," Mrs.

Travilla said, with emotion; for the sad story had deeply touched her heart.

The mournful eyes turned upon her with a grateful look, then closed in the sleep of utter exhaustion.

She passed away that night very calmly and peacefully, trusting in her Redeemer; and as Mildred gazed upon the solemn scene she thanked God that she had been permitted to lead one soul to Him, to smooth one dying pillow, and that Heaven would make amends to the sorely tried one, for all she had been called upon to endure on earth.

Chapter Nineteenth.

"A lovely being, scarcely formed or molded,
A rose with all its sweetest leaves yet folded."
—BYRON.

ON the veranda of a lordly mansion over looking a velvety lawn of emerald green, spangled with flowers and dotted here and there with giant oaks, magnolias and orange trees, between which might be caught the silvery gleam of the bright waters of a lakelet beyond, a young child, a lovely little girl of four, was sporting with her nurse: tossing to and fro a many, colored ball with many a sweet baby laugh and shout.

Presently it flew over the railing and rolled away among the flowers in the grass.

"Let's go get it, mammy," said the little one, hurrying down the steps; "let' stoss it on the lawn."

"Wait, honey," returned the nurse, follow..

ing her. " Ki! let ole mammy hol' you up to see what's comin' down dar on de wattah."

" Oh, the boat, the boat!" shouted the child, as Aunt Chloe lifted her to her shoulder. " Will it stop, mammy? Is uncle comin' on it?"

" Dunno, darlin'; 'spect he is," Aunt Chloe answered moving on across the lawn in the direction of the little pier where the boat was already rounding to. " Ki! yes, dar he am, standin' on de deck."

The child clapped her pretty hands with a cry of delight. " I see him! I see him! Please go on, mammy. Now let me down. I want to run to meet him."

A man was stepping ashore, gentlemanly in dress and appearance, of medium height, rather stoutly built, sandy hair and whiskers, plentifully sprinkled with grey, a grave, thoughtful face, with stern mouth, but kindly grey eyes.

At sight of the fairy little figure bounding toward him, he set down a valise he carried, stooped and held out his arms, the stern lips relaxing into a smile, the grey eyes twinkling.

In an instant she was clinging about his neck, the rosebud mouth pressing sweet kisses on his lips.

" Well, my bonny bairn, are you glad to see your old uncle come home?" he asked, fondling her for a moment; then setting her on her feet and taking her hand, he walked on toward the house, Aunt Chloe and a negro boy with the valise, following.

A pleasant-faced matron, in a neat muslin dress and cap, met them on the veranda.

"Welcome home, sir, Mr. Cameron, "she said shaking hands with him. "Your room's a' ready, and tea will be on the table in ten minutes. Elsie, my bonnie pet, will ye no stay wi' me while uncle changes his linen?"

"Yes, Mrs. Murray, wis you and mammy," the child answered, with cheerful acquiescence. "Uncle won't go 'way to-morrow nor nex' day, 'cause he said so."

The child's meals were usually taken alone in the nursery, earlier hours than those preferred by the older people better suiting her tender years; but to-night she took tea with her guardian and Mr. Murray, Mrs. Murray sitting opposite him and presiding over the tea urn, Elsie between them at his right hand; while Aunt Chloe stood at the back of her chair, ready to give instant attention to every want and wish.

The evenings were cool enough to make an open wood fire very agreeable, and a fine one blazed and crackled on the hearth in the library, whither Mr. Cameron bent his steps on leaving the table.

He had scarcely taken possession of an easy chair beside it, when Elsie crept to his side and claimed a seat on his knee.

"Poor bit fatherless bairn!" he muttered, as he took her up. "Some folk are, as the good book says, 'without natural affection.'"

"Why, uncle, I's dot a papa, hasn't I?" she asked, catching in an understanding way only the first half of his remark; "Mrs. Murray tells me 'bout him sometimes."

"Yes; so you have," he said, "but he isn't here to take care of his little lassie, you know."

"I wis' he was! I wis' he'd come dus' now!

"And my mamma in heaven where Jesus is," she prattled on, "my sweet, pretty mamma," and pulling at a gold chain about her neck, she drew out from the bosom of her gown a miniature set in gold and diamonds, a likeness of a very beautiful young girl.

"Dear mamma, sweet, pretty mamma!" she repeated, fondly kissing the pictured face.

"Let me look at it, Elsie," he said, as she was about to return it to its hiding place.

"The bonniest face I ever saw," he mused half aloud, gazing intently upon it. "Woe's

me that the sods of the valley shou.d ha' cov
ered it from sight sae soon! Was I wrong!
Eh, how could I know that she cared so much
for that wild youth? I thought it was the
gowd he was after, and I think so still."

But he heaved a profound remorseful sigh,
as he relinquished the miniature to its rightful
owner.

As he did so he caught sight of Aunt Chloe
standing near, her dark eyes fixed on him with
an expression of keenest sorrow, mingled with
reproach.

"She blames me," he thought uneasily.
"Well, well, I meant it all for the best."

"Aunt Chloe," he said, speaking aloud,
"bring me a parcel you'll find on my dressing
table."

She left the room, and presently returned
bringing what he had sent her for.

"Something for you, Elsie," he said, lay
ing it in her lap.

It was loosely wrapped in brown paper
which she quickly unfolded with her small
white fingers, bringing to light a large, beautiful and handsomely-dressed doll.

"Oh, oh! see, mammy, see!" she cried in delight; "such a big dolly! biggest of all I's dot!"

Then she thanked the giver with kisses and

smiles and sweet words of baby gratitude; for she was a child of most grateful and loving disposition.

Mrs. Murray must be called in to see and admire the new treasure; then with it hugged closely in her arms, the delighted darling bade good-night and suffered her mammy to lead her away to bed.

"What a bonny wean it is! One canna think well o' the father that neglects it," remarked Mr. Cameron, as the tiny, fairy-like figure disappeared through the doorway.

"It's unaccountable, and whiles makes me hae grave doubts of the reality of his love for the mother," said the housekeeper. "But if once he got sight o' the bairn it would surely be different. Who could see the bit winsome thing and not love her dearly? Can ye no manage to get him here by hook or by crook, Mr. Cameron?"

"I cannot say that I'm over anxious," he answered drily. "He's too fiery and hot-headed a youth to deal comfortably with; besides he's away in Europe."

"Ah! when will he return?"

"Indeed, Mrs. Murray, I got no hint o' that, except that his stay was likely to be lengthy."

She had brought in her accounts of household expenditures for the past month, and some time was spent in going over them and conversing of various business matters.

"Mr. Cameron," she said, as the interview was about to close, "life and health are both uncertain wi' us all. In case onything should happen to you, sir, what—"

"I will give you the address of my solicitor, and o' the bairn's grandfather," he said, without waiting for the conclusion of her sentence ; and turning to his writing desk he wrote both on a card, which he handed to her, saying, "It would be advisable for you, or the overseer, to send them both word immediately if aught occur to deprive me of the ability to attend to the affairs o' the estate and the welfare o' the bit lassie."

Scarce a week had elapsed when Mrs. Murray found reason to be thankful for this act of prudent foresight. Mr. Cameron was taken suddenly and violently ill, soon became delirious, and after a few days of suffering, breathed his last, without an interval in which he could have attended to business, however important.

As soon as it was known that the illness was likely to terminate fatally, letters were dispatched to the addresses given.

The lawyer living no further away than

New Orleans, was able to reach Viamede in time for the funeral; but it would take weeks for the letter to Mr. Dinsmore to wend its way to Roselands.

Little Elsie saw nothing of her guardian after he was taken sick; she was not shown the corpse, and during the funeral her nurse had her away in a distant part of the grounds.

"She's too young to be saddened wi' thoughts o' death and the grave," said Mrs. Murray; "we'll just tell her, when she asks for her uncle, that he's gone to the beautiful heaven where the Saviour is; and her sweet, pretty mamma, too. And she'll hae only pleasant thoughts about it, the darling pet!"

The good woman had a very strong, motherly affection for the lovely little one, and was more concerned in regard to the possible, not to say probable, separation from her, consequent upon Mr. Cameron's death, than with any other question touching her own earthly future. She did not know what disposal would be made of the child, but was resolved not to endure separation if it could be avoided, even by a considerable pecuniary sacrifice.

The lawyer could tell her nothing except that the child's father would now assume entire control of both her person and property.

"Then," she said with the tears stealing down her cheeks, "I fear we may have to part; but I will ever comfort myself with the thought that God reigns and the mon's heart is in His hand as the rivers of water; so that He can turn it whithersoever He will."

"You seem strongly attached to her," remarked the lawyer. "Well, she's a pretty little creature and a great heiress; the estate was large at the time of the grandfather's death, and has flourished under my friend Cameron's care; his investments were always judicious. In fact he couldn't have handled the funds more wisely and carefully if it had been his own. Mr. Dinsmore has been sent for, you say?"

"The grandfather, sir; the father's away in Europe."

"Ah! rather unfortunate, I fear. Well, Mrs. Murray, I have finished the business that brought me here, and shall leave by the next boat; which passes, I understand, half an hour from this," he concluded, consulting his watch.

"Yes," she said; "but you will first step into the dining-room and take some refreshment, will you not, sir? It is quite ready."

He accepted the invitation, and while sipping his tea, said, "I shall see Mr. Dinsmore in New Orleans; he will doubtless call upon me there before coming on to Viamede, and you may depend, Mrs. Murray, that if I have any influence it will be exerted in favor of the plan of leaving the little girl in your care."

" I thank you, sir," she said. " I love the sweet bairn as I loved my own, now all gone before to the heavenly rest, and perhaps, as they hae never seemed to care to trouble wi' her, they may be willing to continue her in my charge."

Mrs. Murray was by no means the only one at Viamede who dreaded the changes that might come as an indirect consequence of the death of Elsie's guardian; there were many anxious hearts among the older and more intelligent of the servants. Would the little mistress, whom they fairly idolized, be carried away from them? Would there be a change of overseers? Would any of them be sold away from home and kindred?

Work had been suspended on account of the funeral. It was over, and returning to their accustomed haunts about the mansion and the quarter, they collected in little groups here and there, looking sadly into each other's faces, talking in subdued tones, with many a dubious shake of the head, and not a few tears dropped to the memory of the fair young creature who had left them four years agone to lie down beside her parents in the family burial ground on a grassy slope not far away.

Ah, could they but have kept her ! so sweet, so gentle, so kind.

Presently Aunt Chloe and her young charge, taking the quarter on their way to the mansion, appeared among them, the baby girl looking wondrously like to her whom they mourned; the same fair, oval face, large, lustrous brown eyes, golden brown hair and sunny smile.

They gathered about her with honeyed words of endearments, kissing the small white hands, the golden ringlets, even the hem of her richly embroidered white dress ; she scattering gracious winsome words and smiles like a little queen among her loyal subjects.

It was truly the homage of the heart, for scarce one of them would have hesitated to risk life and limb in her service.

She dispensed her favors with great impartiality, and was borne to the house on the shoulders of several of these ardent admirers, each taking his turn in carrying her part of the way, that all might share in the privilege ; since the loving little heart would not favor one to the rejection of the others.

It was just as Mr. Coonly, the solicitor, was

about taking his departure that the baby girl was thus borne in triumph to the veranda, and set down there all flushed and rosy and crowing with delight.

"Nice ride, Uncle Ben, and all you other uncles," she said, kissing her hand to them. "Mammy will get you some cakes."

"She's a beautiful child!" exclaimed the solicitor in an aside to Mrs. Murray.

"Yes, sir; and a dear bairn, sweet and good as she is fair."

"Will you give me a good-bye kiss, my little dear?" he asked, stepping toward her.

"Yes," she said, holding up her rosebud mouth. "But I don't know you. Did you come to see my uncle? Where is he?"

He gave her a puzzled look, then saying, "I haven't time to tell you now, my little girl," hurried away.

She looked after him for a moment, then turning to Mrs. Murray, repeated her question.

"Gone away, darling," was the answer "Now come in and eat your supper; and then we'll have a nice bit talk."

Chapter Twentieth.

" Not mine—yet dear to me—fair, fragrant blossom
Of a fair tree—
Crushed to the earth in life's first glorious summer,—
Thou'rt dear to me,
Child of the lost, the buried and the sainted."
—MRS. WELBY.

THE housekeeper's room, to which she now led the little Elsie, was a cheery, pleasant place. On a small round table, covered with snowy satin-like damask, and a service of glittering silverware, cut glass and Sevres china, a tempting little repast was laid out for the two.

Mrs. Murray took her seat, and Aunt Chloe lifted Elsie into a high chair opposite.

The little one closed her eyes, folded her baby hands and bent reverently over her plate, while Mrs. Murray asked, in a few simple words, a blessing on their food.

Aunt Chloe waited on them while they ate, devoting herself particularly to her infant charge, as another servant was in attendance, then withdrew to the servants' hall to eat her own supper.

And now Mrs. Murray, seating herself in a low rocking-chair, took the child on her lap.

Elsie nestled in her arms, laid her head on her shoulder, and softly patting her cheek, said, " I love you, Mrs. Murray."

" I dinna doubt it, my sweet, bit lassie, and I love you too ; dearly, dearly," the good woman returned, accompanying the words with tender, motherly caresses. " And the dear Lord Jesus loves you better still, darling. Never forget that, never doubt that you are His own precious lambkin, and that He is always near to hear you when you pray."

" Yes, I know," answered the child, " Jesus loves little children, Jesus loves little Elsie. And some day He'll let Elsie go to live wis Him and wis her sweet, pretty mamma. Jesus loves my mamma, and lets her live 'long wis Him."

" Yes, dear, she is there in that happy land. And uncle has gone to be with her now."

The child started, lifted up her head, and gazing earnestly, questioningly into the house-keeper's eyes, asked, " Uncle gone too ? Will he come back again ? "

" No, dear bairn, they never want to come back from that blessed land ; they are so happy there with the dear Saviour."

" Why didn't he take Elsie 'long ? " cried

the child, bursting into tears; "I want to go dere too."

"Jesus didn't send for you this time, sweet pet," the housekeeper answered with emotion, and folding the little form closer to her heart; "He would have you and me bide here yet a bit; but some day He will call us home too. He's getting a very lovely home ready for us there."

"For my papa too?"

"I trust so, darling."

"Where is my papa? why doesn't he come to Elsie."

"I don't know, my bonnie bairn. I think he will come some day."

"And take Elsie on his knee, and kiss her and love her?"

"Surely, surely, darling. And you have a grandpa, who will be here before many days, I trust."

"Grandpa that's gone to heaven?"

"No; that is Grandpa Grayson, your sweet mamma's father; this is Grandpa Dinsmore, your papa's father."

The child looked thoughtful for a moment, then with a joyous smile exclaimed, "Elsie's so glad! I wish he'd come now. Elsie will love him ever so much."

"May the Lord open his heart to love you in return, sweet bairnie," sighed the good woman. "But not to take you frae me," she added mentally.

The child pleaded for "stories 'bout mamma; Elsie's mamma when she was little girlie, and played wis her little brothers and sisters."

Mrs. Murray having been housekeeper at Viamede for nearly twenty years, had a plentiful store of these laid up in her memory. Each one had been repeated for the little girl's entertainment a score of times or more, but repetition seemed to have no power to lessen their interest for her.

"Why doesn't Elsie have brothers and sisters?" she asked during a pause in the narration. "Elsie do want some so bad!"

"Our Father didna see fit to give you any, dear bairn; and so you must try to be content without," Mrs. Murray answered, with a tender caress; "we canna have all we would like in this world; but when we get home where the dear Lord Jesus is, we'll have nothing left to wish for; our cup o' joy will be full to overflowing. Now bid me good-night, my wee bonnie, bonnie darling, for here's mammy come to take you to bed."

The child complied with alacrity. She and

her mammy were devotedly attached to each other, and had seldom been apart for an hour since the little girl first saw the light.

And the nurse, though wholly uneducated, was as simple-hearted and earnest a Christian as Mrs. Murray herself, and faithfully carried out the dying injunction of the young mother, to try to teach her little one, from her earliest years, to love and fear the Lord.

She talked and sang to her of Jesus before she was a year old, and as soon as she began to speak, taught her to kneel night and morning with folded hands and lisp her little prayer. And she, too, told her sweet stories of the mother she had never known, of the beautiful home whither she had gone, of the loving Saviour who was with her there, and also on earth watching over her darling.

Every night she rocked her to sleep in her arms, soothing her to rest with these ever new stories, and the sweet wild melodies common among her race.

Aunt Chloe had known sorrows many and bitter, not the least of them the untimely death of Elsie's mother, and with none left to her in whose veins her own blood flowed, clung to this nursling with a love that would have hesitated at no sacrifice for the good of its object, a passion-

ate, yearning tenderness that would have led
her to choose death for herself rather than separation. The big tears chased each other down
her sable cheeks at the bare thought of such a
possibility, as she held her sleeping treasure in
her arms that night.

She knew little of the child's father, noth·
ing whatever of the grandfather or any other
of the paternal relatives, and her heart misgave
her lest there might be trouble in store for herself and her beloved charge.

Some one came in softly through the open
door, and Chloe looked up with the tears still on
her cheeks, to find the housekeeper close at her
side. "What is it, Aunt Chloe?" she asked, in
a tone of alarm; "the dear bairn is not ill?"

Chloe only shook her head, while her
bosom heaved with half-suppressed sobs.

"Ah, I know what it is!" sighed Mrs.
Murray; "your heart trembles wi' the vera same
fear that oppresses mine:—lest the darling o'
our dear love be torn frae our arms. But we
winna greet for sorrow that may never come ·
we winna doubt His love and power who doeth
all things well. Let us no forget that He loves
her better far than we do.

"Said the saintly Rutherford, 'I shall charge
my soul to believe and to wait for Him, and

shall follow His providence, and not go before it, nor stay behind it.' Let us make the same resolve, Aunt Chloe, and be happy while we may ; be happy alway ; for His loving kindness shall never fail.

"Dinna ye mind his word, ' I am the Lord who exercise loving kindness, judgment and righteousness in the earth ; for in these things I delight, saith the Lord ? ' "

"Ef dey take my bressed lamb away, dis ole heart break for sure!" sobbed Chloe, clasping the child closer. "I's done gone los' eberyting else !"

"No, no, Aunt Chloe! not the Lord !"

"No, missus, not de Lord ! dat true. Hope He forgib de sinful word ! "

"And not the hope of heaven !"

"No, no, missus, not dat either, bress His holy name !"

"It is a world of trial, Aunt Chloe, but He never sends one that is na needful for us ; and ' when His people cannot have a providence of silk and roses, they must be content with such an one as he carveth out for them.' ' How soon would grace freeze without a cross !' "

"Dat true, missus; an' we mus' take de cross first or we can't hab de crown at de las'," she assented with a heavy sigh. " Missus, do you

know what gwine be done now? will dey sell
de plantation?"

"Oh, no! it belongs to the bairn."

"De servants?"

"I don't think there is any danger o' that
either; for they, too, are hers."

Aunt Chloe breathed more freely. "Will
Massa Dinsmore come an' lib heyah hisself?"
she asked.

"That I canna tell," Mrs. Murray said, shaking her head and sighing slightly. "But,
Aunt Chloe, I dinna think ye need fear bein'
parted frae the bairn. They may take her frae
me, but they'll no be likely to separate her
from her mammy; wherever she goes you will,
in a' probability, go also."

Chloe asked if Elsie was to be taken away
from Viamede; to which the housekeeper answered that she did not know; indeed, nothing
could be known till Mr. Dinsmore came.

"But," she added, "whether the sweet
bairn's home be here or elsewhere, an attendant
will be needed, and I see no reason why the old
mammy, who loves her sae dearly, should be exchanged for another. I wad be blithe to think
myself as secure o' bein' kept near her; but
they're no sae likely to want a housekeeper as a
nurse, should they decide to change her abode."

"'Tank de Lord for dat!" ejaculated **Aunt Chloe**, half under her breath, as she rose and gently laid the sleeping child in her bed. "I tink my bressed lamb neber be happy widout her ole mammy to lub her, an' I hopes dey'll let you stay too, missus. I'e afraid Massa Dinsmore not care much 'bout his little chile; 'cause ef he do, why he neber come for to see her?"

The words sounded to Mrs. Murray like the echo of her own thoughts.

"I dinna understand it," she whispered, bending over the little one to press a tender kiss on the softly rounded, rosy cheek. "I canna comprehend it; but the sweet wean has had a happy life thus far, and please God, **Aunt Chloe**, she'll ne'er want for love while he leaves her in our care."

Chapter Twenty-first.

"A sweet, heartlifting cheerfulness,
Like springtime of the year,
Seemed ever on her steps to wait."
—MRS. HALE.

"I SHOULD like to have a little chat with you, Milly, my dear," Mr. Dinsmore said pleasantly, looking across the table at her, where she sat behind the tea urn; her accustomed place now in Mrs. Dinsmore's absence; "can you give me an hour or two of your company, in the library, this evening?"

"Just as much of it as you may happen to want, uncle," she answered brightly.

"Thank you," he said. "I rejoice every day in having you here; it would be extremely dull without you. But I wonder sometimes how you keep up your spirits. Nearly six weeks since Mrs. Dinsmore went away, and nobody in the house, the greater part of the time, but yourself, the housekeeper and servants."

"It is a little lonely sometimes," she ac-

knowledged, " but I have you at meals and in
the evenings, generally, now and then a call
from one of the neighbors, and almost every
day 1 ride over to Ion and spend an hour or
two with dear Mrs. Travilla. So with the assistance of books, music and drawing, and writing
letters to mother and the rest, I find the days
pass quite rapidly."

" Ah! there is a great deal in being disposed to be contented !" he said, smiling. " You
are like your mother in that, too.

" We have not yet succeeded in finding a
suitable person to fill Miss Worth's place, and
that is one reason your aunt gives for lingering
so long at her sister's. The place affords excellent educational advantages."

There was a little more desultory chat, and
then, having finished their meal, they repaired
to the library, Mildred not a little curious to
learn what her uncle had to say; for she felt
quite certain from his manner that it was something of unusual importance.

He drew an easy chair to the fire, seated her
comfortably therein, then turning away, paced
the floor for some moments in silence, and with
an abstracted air and clouded brow.

She watched him furtively, wondering more
and more at his evident disturbance.

At last, heaving a profound sigh, he seated himself near her.

"You are already acquainted, Mildred, so your Aunt Wealthy informed me," he began, in the tone of one who approaches a very distasteful subject, "with a certain chapter in my son Horace's history, which I would be exceedingly glad to bury in forgetfulness; but that circumstances have rendered impossible—since the child of that most imprudent, ill-advised marriage has seen fit to live, and of course her existence cannot be entirely ignored."

Mildred was growing indignant. Her color heightened and her eyes sparkled; though unperceived by him, as his face was half averted.

"Is there anything wrong with her, uncle?" she ventured as he came to a pause.

"Wrong with her?" he echoed. "Heaven forbid! It is bad enough as it is. But, indeed, I have never taken the trouble to ask. In fact, I believe I half unconsciously hoped she might never cross my path. But," and again he sighed, "that is past. A letter received this morning from Louisiana, brings news of the death of her guardian—that is, you understand, the man who was left guardian to her mother and the property; which, by the way, is very large."

Mildred began to listen with eager interest
She had wished very much to see Horace's
child ; could it be that that wish was to be
gratified ?

"The child heirs it all," Mr. Dinsmore
went on. "The mother married and died
under age, and by the conditions of the will
the property remained in Mr. Cameron's care ;
the child also, Horace not caring to remove
her. Now, however, the responsibility all falls
upon me, in his absence. I must look after
both estate and heiress. It involves an immediate journey to Louisiana, probably a stay of
some weeks, to get matters settled.

"And I must bring the child home with
me, as of course leaving her there with servants
only is not to be thought of, and, in fact, I know
of no other home for her ; for being a mere
babe she cannot be sent to boarding-school.

"I anticipate some complaint from Mrs.
Dinsmore ; she will not like it, I know, but it
really cannot be helped, and need not add to
her cares in the least."

"Poor little motherless thing !" sighed Mildred softly, and as Mr. Dinsmore gave her a hasty
glance he saw that her eyes were full of tears.

"It is a pity about her," he said. "Strange
that she was destined to survive her mother ;

it would really have been so much more com
fortable for all parties if she had not."

"It does seem as though it might have been
happy thing for her," Mildred answered
drily.

But he did not notice the tone. Turning
to her with a smile, "How would you like to go
with me to Louisiana?" he asked.

Her face grew radiant with delight at the
bare suggestion. "O, uncle! how delightful!
But it would be a very expensive journey,
wouldn't it?" and her countenance fell.

"That would be my concern, since I invite
you," he said, laughing and playfully tapping
her cheek. "Where did you learn to be so
careful and economical? Don't trouble yourself about expense. I shall consider the pleasure of your company cheaply purchased at the
cost of settling all the bills. Now will you go?"

"Yes, indeed, and thank you a thousand
times! if—"

"If what? father and mother give consent!
There's no time to ask it, as I leave day after
to-morrow; but I am sure it would not be with-
held. So we'll do as we please first and ask
permission afterward."

"Yes," Mildred responded, after a moment's
musing, "I feel convinced that they would be

very glad to have me accept your kind, generous offer; for it is such an opportunity as I am not likely to meet with again."

The remainder of the evening was devoted to the writing of a long, bright and cheery letter to her mother, telling of the pleasant prospect before her, and promising that the home circle should share in the enjoyments of her trip so far as descriptions of scenery and adventures, written in her best style, could enable them to do.

Mildred's letters had come to be considered a very great treat in that little community their reception looked forward to with eager anticipation. The enjoyment would be doubled when they told of scenes new and fascinating, and of Cousin Horace's little girl, in whom they already felt so deep an interest.

Mildred had enjoyed her visit to Roselands but since the death of Miss Worth the atmosphere of the house had seemed somewhat lonely and depressing. So she was very glad of her uncle's invitation; which promised a change in every way delightful.

The journey was tedious and wearisome in those days, compared to what it would be now—staging across the country to the nearest point on the Mississippi, thence by steamboat to New Orleans, where they remained several weeks, Mr. Dinsmore being engaged in making necessary arrangements in regard to that portion of little Elsie's inheritance which lay in the Crescent City; then on to Viamede.

It pleased Mildred that this part of their trip was to be all the way by water, and after they entered Teche Bayou it seemed to her like a passage through fairy land, so bright were the skies, so balmy the breezes, so rich and varied was the scenery; swamps, forest, plain, gliding by in rapid succession, the eye roving over the richest vegetation; resting now upon some cool, shady dell gayly carpeted with flowers, now on a lawn covered with velvet-like grass of emerald green, and nobly shaded by magnificent oaks and magnolias, now catching sight of a lordly villa peeping through its groves of orange trees, and anon of a tall white sugar house, or a long row of cabins, the homes of the laborers.

It was a new region of country to Mr. Dinsmore as well as herself, and he remarked that he considered the sight of it a sufficient recompense of itself for the trouble and expense of the journey.

"But beside that," he added, "I have had the satisfaction of learning that the estate is even much larger than I supposed. That Scotchman was faithful to his trust; very shrewd, too, in making investments, and his death gives Horace control, during the child's minority, of a princely income."

"Then you do not regret his marriage so much as you did?" Mildred said inquiringly.

"I do not say that," was the cold, almost stern reply; and she said no more.

Chapter Twenty-second.

"I would that thou might'st ever be
As beautiful as now ;
That time might ever leave as free
Thy yet unwritten brow."

—WILLIS.

"WHEN will my grandpa come ?" little Elsie asked again and again, and finding that no one could tell her, she set herself to watch the passing boats, often coaxing her mammy out upon the lawn or down to the very water's edge, in her eagerness for a sight of him ; her first look into the face of a relative.

She was fond of Mrs. Murray as she had been of Mr. Cameron, and clung with ardent affection to her mammy, yet the baby heart yearned for parental love, and naturally she expected it from her grandfather.

Had she heard that her father was coming, she would have been wild with joy ; the arrival of her grandfather seemed the next best thing that could happen.

Mildred knew nothing of the child's anticipations, yet her heart ached for the little creature as she perceived how determined Mr. Dinsmore was to shut her out from his.

"She's a fortunate little miss," he remarked of her, as they came in sight of a sugar and orange plantation exceeding in size and fertility almost any they had passed, and the captain of the boat, pointing it out, said, "That's Viamede; the old Grayson place."

They were sweeping by a large sugar house; then came an immense orange orchard, and then a long and wide stretch of lawn, with the loveliest carpet of velvety green and most magnificent shade trees they had ever beheld; half concealing, with their great arms and abundant foliage, a lordly mansion set far back among them.

So surpassingly lovely was the whole scene, that for a moment Mildred could have echoed her uncle's words, and almost found it in her heart to envy the young heiress of it all; but the next she said to herself, "No, no, not for all this would I be so lonely and loveless as she, poor, little, forlorn girlie!"

The boat rounded to at the little pier. Close by, in the shade of a great oak, stood an elderly colored woman with a child in her arms—a little girl of fairy-like form, and face perfect in out-line and feature, a complexion of dazzling bril-liance, a countenance radiant with delight—as she watched the travelers stepping ashore.

"This is she, I presume," Mr. Dinsmore said coolly, halting in front of the two. "What's your name, child?"

"Elsie Dinsmore," she answered, her lip quivering, the large soft eyes filling with tears. "I fought it was my grandpa comin'."

"And so it is," he said, slightly touched by her evident disappointment. "Have you a kiss for me?"

For answer she threw both arms about his neck, as he bent toward her, and pressed her red lips to his.

He disengaged himself rather hastily, step-ping back to give place to Mildred, who, gazing with delight upon the beautiful little creature, was eagerly awaiting her turn.

"You darling!" she cried, clasping the child in a warm embrace. "This is Cousin Milly; and she is going to love you dearly, dearly!"

"Tank you, Miss," said Aunt Chloe, with tears in her eyes. "And welcome to Viamede, Miss; welcome, Massa," dropping a courtesy to each.

Mrs. Murray and several servants now came hurrying toward them; there were more courtesies and welcomes; the baggage was seized and quick.y transported to the house; the travelers, Mrs. Murray, and Aunt Chloe with her little charge, following it leisurely.

Mildred was filled with delight at the beauty surrounding her, yet more attracted by the child than by all else. She turned toward her with an affectionate smile, and the little one, now walking by her nurse's side, returning it with one of rare sweetness, ran to her and slipped a tiny, soft, white hand into hers.

"Is she not beautiful, uncle?" Mildred asked with enthusiasm, at the first opportunity for doing so without being overheard.

"She's no Dinsmore," he said coldly; "not a trace of Horace's looks about her; must be all Grayson, I presume."

"Oh, how can he!" thought Mildred, "how can he harden his heart so against anything so gentle and beautiful!"

They were standing on the veranda for a moment, admiring the view and watching the departure of the boat which had brought them; while Mrs. Murray was busied in giving directions in regard to the disposal of their luggage.

A suit of delightful apartments had been

appropriated to Mildred's use during her stay.
Conducted thither by Aunt Chloe and her
nursling, she took possession with great content, and with the assistance of a skilled waiting maid, also placed at her service, soon
arrayed her neat figure in a becoming dinner
dress, little Elsie and her mammy looking on
admiringly the while.

"Isn't my cousin *so* pretty, mammy?"
whispered the little one.

Mildred heard, and turning with a pleased
smile, held out her hand to the child. "Won't
you come and sit on cousin's lap a little while?
I can tell you about your dear papa; for I
know him."

The child's face grew radiant, and she hastened to accept the invitation.

"Oh," she said, "please do! Will he come
here soon? I want to see my papa! I want to
kiss him and love him."

The soft eyes filled with tears, and the red
lips quivered.

Mildred clasped the little form close in her
arms and kissed the sweet, fair face over and
over, exclaiming in tremulous tones, "You
dear, precious baby! if he could only see you,
I'm sure he couldn't help loving you with all
his heart!"

The travelers were summoned to the dinner table, and little Elsie partook with them,
conducting herself with the utmost propriety.

"She seems a well-behaved child," her
grandfather remarked graciously. "How old
are you, my dear? can you tell?"

"I's four," piped the bird-like voice; "I's a
big girl now, grandpa; too big to be naughty;
but sometimes I's not very good."

"Ah! that's honest," he said, with an
amused smile. "Well, what do they do to you
when you're naughty?"

"When I was a little girl, mammy put me
in de corner sometimes."

"And what now you are so large?"

"She jus' say, 'Jesus not pleased wis my
darlin' child, when she naughty.'"

"But you don't mind that, do you?" he
asked curiously.

She looked at him with innocent, wondering eyes. "Elsie loves Jesus; Elsie wants
Jesus to love her and make her His little lamb;
she asks Him to do it every day."

"Stuff!" he muttered, in a tone of annoyance; but tears of joy and thankfulness wel ed
up in Mildred's eyes.

"Blessed baby!" she thought, "you will
not have a lonely, loveless life if you have so

soon begun to seek the dear Saviour. Ah, how my mother's heart will rejoice to hear this!"

On coming to the table the little one had folded her tiny hands, and bending with closed eyes over her plate, murmured a short grace; but Mr. Dinsmore, busying himself in carving a fowl, did not seem to notice it; yet it had not escaped him; he was watching the child furtively, and with far more interest than he would have liked to own.

"I'm afraid they're making a canting hypocrite of her," he said to Mildred when they had retired to the drawing-room.

"O, uncle, do not say that!" exclaimed Mildred. "It is just the way my dear mother, whom you admire so much, trains and teaches her children."

"Ah!" he said, "then I shall have to retract."

"What pretty manners she has, uncle; both at the table and elsewhere," remarked Mildred; "she handles knife, fork and spoon as deftly as possible, and is so gentle and refined in all she does and says."

"Yes," he said with some pride, "I trust an uncouth, ill-mannered Dinsmore might be considered an anomaly, indeed."

" Then you acknowledge that she is a **Dins-more ?**" Mildred said playfully.

"Have I ever denied that she was Horace's child ?" he answered with a smile.

" I wish he could see her at this moment. I am sure he could not help feeling that he had good reason to be proud of her," Mildred said, approaching a window that looked out upon the lawn, where the little one was wandering about gathering flowers ; " see, uncle ! is not every movement full of grace ?"

"You seem to be quite bewitched with her," he returned, good humoredly, following the direction of her glance. " Children's movements are not apt to be ungraceful, I think.

" This is a fine old mansion," he went on, " and seems to be well furnished throughout. Have you been in the library ? No ? Then come ; we will visit it now. Your heart will rejoice at sight of the well-filled book shelves.

" Ah, I knew it ! " watching the expression of keen satisfaction with which she regarded them, when he had taken her there.

They consisted largely of very valuable works in every branch of literature, and Mildred's sole regret was that she would have so little time to examine and enjoy them.

There were also some few fine paintings

and beautiful pieces of statuary in the room, and indeed scattered through all the principal rooms of the house; the drawing-room being especially rich in them.

They lingered for some time over these works of art, then went out upon the veranda, presently wandering on from that to the lawn, where they strolled about a little, and finally seated themselves under a beautiful magnolia.

" Ah, see what a pretty picture they make ! " Mildred exclaimed, glancing in the direction of another, at some little distance, in whose shade Aunt Chloe was seated upon the grass with Elsie in her lap, both busied with the flowers they had been gathering.

" Yes," said Mr. Dinsmore ; " and what a striking contrast! the child so young, and delicately fair, the nurse so black and elderly ; she seems much attached to her charge."

" Yes, indeed ! You do not think of separating them, uncle ? "

" Certainly not ! why should I ? "

Mildred answered only with a pleased look, for at that moment little Elsie left her mammy and came running with a lovely bouquet in each hand.

" One for you, grandpa, and one for Cousin

Mill/," she said, dropping a graceful little courtesy as she presented them.

"Thank you, dear; how pretty they are!" Mildred said, kissing her.

"Humph! what shall I do with it?" Mr. D.nsmore asked, accepting his.

"Put it in your buttonhole," said the child. "That's the way uncle does."

"Uncle? who is he? You have none that you ever saw, so far as I know."

"Massa Cameron, sah," explained Aunt Chloe, coming up; "he always tole my chile call him dat."

"Well, she needn't do so any more. I don't like it. Do you hear?" to Elsie, "don't call that man uncle again. He was no relation whatever to you."

His tone spoke displeasure, and the little one drew back to the shelter of her mammy's arms, with a frightened look, her lip trembling, her soft, brown eyes full of tears.

"There, there!" he said, more gently, "don't cry; I'm not angry with you; you knew no better."

He rose and wandered away toward the rear of the mansion, and Mildred drew Elsie to a seat upon her lap, caressing her tenderly.

"Sweet little girlie," she said, "cousin loves

you dearly, already, and cannot bear to see tears in those eyes. Tell me about your sweet, pretty mamma."

"Here she is, cousin. Don't you love her too?" prattled the babe, drawing forth the miniature from her bosom, and quickly forgetting her momentary grief in displaying it. "She's gone up to heaven to stay wis Jesus, and some day he'll take Elsie there too."

"Mildred," said Mr. Dinsmore, coming back, "I hear there are fine saddle horses in the stables. If I order two of them brought round, will you ride over the plantation with me?"

"Gladly!" she said, putting the child gently down, and rising with alacrity. "I will go at once and don my riding habit. You shall tell me the rest another time, little pet."

Already enthusiastic admirers of Viamede, they returned from their ride doubly impressed with its beauties.

"It seems an earthly paradise," Mildred wrote to her mother, "and the little owner is the loveliest, most fairy-like little creature you can imagine—so sweet, so gentle, so beautiful! and good as she is pretty. Mrs. Murray tells me she is generosity itself, and she dosen't believe there is a grain of selfishness in her nature. Elsie showed me her mamma's miniature, and

it is so sweet and beautiful that I do not wonder Cousin Horace lost his heart at first
sight."

But it was not until the next day that this
letter was written. Mildred had enough to do
that day in looking about her and making acquaintance with Elsie and her attendants.

After tea, Mr. Dinsmore being closeted with
the overseer, she made her way to the nursery,
coaxed the little one into her lap again—though
indeed no great amount of persuasion was
needed—and amused her for an hour or two
with stories and nursery rhymes.

But the child's bedtime drew near, and with
a tender good-night, a lingering, loving caress,
Mildred left her and went down to the drawing-
room.

Her uncle was not there, and passing out to
the veranda, she fell into chat with Mrs. Murray,
whom she found seated there enjoying the beautiful scenery and the soft evening air.

Their talk turned naturally upon Viamede
and the Grayson family; particularly Horace
Dinsmore's wife, the last of the race; Mrs.
Murray giving many details that were of great
interest to her hearer.

"She was very lovely," she said, "baith in
person and in character; a sweet, earnest, child-

like Christian; and the bairn is wonderfully
like her. She seemed to me a lamb of the fold
from her very birth; and nae doot in answer to
the mother's prayers. Ye ken, Miss Keith,
that she lived scarce a week after her babe was
born, and all her anxiety was that it should be
trained up in the nurture and admonition o'
the Lord, her constant prayer that He would be
pleased to mak' it His own.

"The bit bairnie isna perfect, of course, but
quite as near it as grown folk. It's very evident
that she tries to please the blessed Saviour;
that she grieves when she has done wrong, and
canna rest till she's been awi' by hersel' to beg
His forgiveness.

"I tell her whiles aboot the new heart God
gives to his children, and that He will give it to
a' such as ask earnestly; and she will look up
in my face with those great innocent eyes and
answer, 'Yes, Mrs. Murray; and I do ask
earnestly every day'."

The old lady brushed away a tear, and her
voice was slightly tremulous as she added, " Mr.
Cameron used to fret a bit whiles, lest she was
too gude to live:—like her mother before her,
he wad say. But I canna think early piety
any sign that life will be short. Except, indeed, that when the work o' grace is fully done

glory follows. She's come o' a God-fearing race, Miss Keith, and the Lord's aye faithful to His promise ;—showing mercy to thousands o' generations o' them that love Him and keep His commandments.

Chapter Twenty-third

As Mildred sat at the open window of her dressing-room the next morning, enjoying the beauty of the landscape, the delicious perfume of myriads of dew-laden shrubs and flowers, the gentle summer breeze and the glad songs of the birds, her ear caught the patter of little feet in the corridor without, then a gentle rap upon her door.

She made haste to open it, and a vision of loveliness met her view :—a tiny, fairy form arrayed in spotless white, of some thin, delicate fabric, trimmed with costly lace, and a broad sash of pale blue, with slippers to match; a shining mass of golden brown curls clustering about the sweet face and rippling over the fair neck and shoulders.

The soft brown eyes looked up lovingly into

her face, and the rosebud mouth was held up
for a kiss.

"Good morning, cousin," said the bird-like
voice; "do Elsie 'sturb you coming so soon?"

"No, darling, indeed you don't!" cried
Mildred, giving her a rapturous embrace; "I
can't see too much of you, dear little pet!
Will you come and sit in my lap while we have
another nice talk?"

The child hesitated. "Don't you want to
come wis me, cousin, and see my mamma when
she was a little girl, and my mamma's things?"

"I should like it greatly," Mildred answered, suffering herself to be led along the
corridor and into an open door at its farther
end.

Here she found herself in a beautiful boudoir; evidently no expense had been spared in
furnishing it in the most luxurious and tasteful
manner; even Mildred's inexperienced eye recognized the costly nature of many of its adorn
ments, though there was nothing gaudy about
them.

Elsie led her directly to a full-length, life-
sized picture of a little girl of ten or twelve,
before which Mildred stood transfixed with de
light,—face and form were so life-like, and so
exquisitely lovely.

She gazed upon it for many minutes with ravished eyes, then glancing at the little one standing by her side, said half aloud, " Beautiful as it is, I do not believe it is flattered ; for it is just what she will be six or eight years hence."

" It's my mamma when she was a little girl," Elsie said, " and this," drawing the miniature from her bosom, "is my mamma when she was a lady."

Mildred gazed upon it again long and earnestly, thinking as before, that there was abundant excuse for her cousin Horace's passion and his inconsolable grief over his loss.

There were two other portraits in the room, which Elsie said were " Grandpa and Grandma Grayson."

She pointed out, too, her mother's writing-desk and her work-table, a dainty basket upon this last, with its little gold thimble and a bit of embroidery with the needle still sticking in it, just as it had been laid down by the white hands on the morning of the day on which the little one first saw the light.

It was Aunt Chloe, coming in in search of her nursling, who told Mildred this.

But Elsie drew her on through a beautiful dressing-room into a spacious and elegantly fur

nished bedroom beyond, and Aunt Chloe following, pointed out, with bitter weeping, the
pillow on which the dying head had lain, and
described the last hours of her idolized young
mistress:—her mournful leave-taking of her
little babe, and dying injunction to her to bring
her up to love the Lord Jesus.

It was all intensely interesting and deeply
affecting to Mildred.

"Don't cry, mammy, you dear ole mammy! '
said Elsie, pulling her nurse down into a chair,
and with her own tiny white handkerchief
wiping away her tears, "don't cry, 'cause dear
mamma is very happy wis Jesus, and you and
Elsie are goin' dere, too, some day. An' den I'll
tell my sweet, pretty mamma you did be good
to her baby, and took care of her all the time."

At that Aunt Chloe strained the tiny form
convulsively to her breast with a fresh burst of
sobs, and looking up at Mildred with the great
tears rolling down her sable cheeks, faltered
out, "O, Miss Milly, dey ain't gwine take my
chile 'way and disseparate ole Chloe from de
las' ting she got lef' to lub in dis world?"

"O, mammy, no, no! dey shan't, dey
shan't!" cried the child, clinging about her neck
in almost wild affright. "Elsie won't go! Elsie
will always stay wis her dear ole mammy!"

" No, no, you are not to be parted," Mildred
hastened to say ; "Elsie, darling, your grandpa
told me you were not.   So don't cry, pet."

" O, Miss Milly, dat bressed news! " cried
Aunt Chloe, smiling through her tears.   " I's
tank you berry much.   Dere, dere, honey darlin', don' cry no mo' !   I's ole fool mammy to
make you cry like dat."

The breakfast bell rang, and hastily remov-
ing the traces of the tears called forth by Aunt
Chloe's narrative, Mildred obeyed the summons.
Mr. Dinsmore seemed in excellent spirits, chat-
ting in quite a lively strain all through the
meal.   He was enchanted with the place, he
said, and intended, if agreeable to Mildred, to
remain some weeks, believing that the change
of scene and climate would prove beneficial to
them both.   Mildred assured him, her eyes
sparkling with delight the while, that she was
perfectly willing to stay as long as suited his
convenience and pleasure.

" There are horses, carriages and servants
always at your command," he remarked; " a
pleasure boat on the lakelet, too, and oarsmen
to row it, so that you can go out on the water,
ride or drive whenever you wish."

" O, uncle, how nice ! " she cried; " I shall
enjoy it all greatly with little Elsie for a com

panion · and you will sometimes go with us
when you have leisure, will you not ? "

" I shall be most happy," he said, " but fear
t wil be but seldom that I can."

The family carriage was ordered at once, and
the greater part of the morning was spent by
Mildred, Elsie and Aunt Chloe in driving from
one lovely spot to another.

At little Elsie's request they visited the
family burial ground, and Mildred viewed with
pensive interest the last resting-place of her
Cousin Horace's young wife—" the sweet, pretty
mamma," of whom the baby girl so constantly
prattled. The spot was beautiful with roses
and many sweet-scented shrubs and flowers
growing there, and daily Elsie and her mammy
came thither with love's offering in the shape
of buds and blossoms gathered from the lawn
and gardens, which they scattered with lavish
hands over each lowly mound, but ever reserv-
ing the most and the loveliest for the grave ot
her whom they loved best.

There was seldom a day when the quarter
was not visited also, Aunt Chloe taking her
nursling from cabin to cabin to inquire concerning the welfare of the inmates, and give to each
the pleasure of the sight of the little fair face
that was so dear to them all.

Their devotion to her, and various ways of manifesting it, greatly pleased and interested Mildred; and she was not long in discovering that they were exceedingly anxious in regard to the question whether both she—their idolized little mistress—and they were to be allowed to remain at Viamede.

Some of them even ventured, in their great anxiety, to inquire of the young lady visitor if she could tell them aught about these things.

She evaded the question so far as it referred to Elsie, feeling that she could not endure the sight of their grief when they should learn that they were to lose her; as to the other part she said, truly, that she was ignorant, but hoped there was no real danger.

She ventured at length to sound her uncle on the subject, telling of the fears of the poor creatures; and to her delight was given liberty to assure them that none would be sold unless unruly and disobedient to orders.

She availed herself of this permission on her next visit to the quarter.

The communication was received with joy and gratitude; but there still remained the great fear that Mr. Dinsmore would carry away their darling; and this Mildred was powerless to remove.

She told Mrs. Murray about it, and the good woman confessed with tears, that she, too, was tortured with the fear of separation from "the sweet bairn she had learned to love as her very own;" asking if Mildred knew whether that trial awaited her.

Mildred looked grieved and perplexed. "I only know," she said, after a moment's hesitation, "that uncle intends taking his little granddaughter home with him. Should you feel willing to leave Viamede, Mrs. Murray?"

"The bairn is far dearer to me than the place; though I hae spent mony o' the best years o' my life here," was the reply. "I wad gang ony where sooner than part frae my bonnie bit lassie. I have a mother's heart for her, Miss Keith, and hae often wanted to bid her call me by some dearer name than Mrs. Murray; but knowing the Dinsmores were proud folk, I feared to offend; and I perceive it was well I refrained, since I hae learned frae Aunt Chloe that the grandfather was no pleased that she spoke o' Mr. Cameron as her uncle."

"No, he didn't seem to like it, and told her not to do so again. But might not that be the jealousy of affection?"

Mildred blushed as she spoke, half ashamed —in view of Mr. Dinsmore's evident lack of

love for the child—of making the suggestion.

"Affection!" repeated Mrs. Murray, with a
faint, incredulous smile; "I dinna see much in
his manner toward the bairn that looks like it."

To this remark Mildred had no answer save
a deeper blush.

But at this moment Mrs. Murray was summoned to a conference with Mr. Dinsmore in
the library. She came back with a face full of
joy and thankfulness.

Mr. Dinsmore had received a letter that day
from Mrs. Brown, the housekeeper at Roselands, saying that her health was failing, the
physician recommended change of climate, and
therefore she must resign her situation for a
year or more.

Mr. Dinsmore now offered it to Mrs. Murray, and Aunt Phillis, an old servant in the
family and every way competent to the task,
would be left in charge of the mansion here.

"I am very glad for both you and little
Elsie," said Mildred, "and yet I feel sorry for
you, and for her, that you must leave this lovely
spot. Is it not a trial?"

"I canna deny that it is," the housekeeper
answered, with a sigh, "for I hae lived at Viamede many years; years in which I hae seen

much o' baith joy and sorrow, and I had hoped
to end my days here; but as the saintly Rutherford says,

" ' This is the Lord's lower house; and
while we are lodged here we have no assurance
to lie ever in one chamber, but must be content
to remove from one Lord's nether house to
another, resting in hope that when we come
up to the Lord's upper city, Jerusalem, that is
above, we shall remove no more; because then
we shall be at home.'   Ah, Miss Milly, what a
joyous day it will be when we win there ! "

Chapter Twenty-fourth.

"Must I leave thee, Paradise ? thus leave
Thee, native soil, these happy walks and shades,
Fit haunts of Gods ?"

—MILTON.

MR. DINSMORE was, in the main, a kind-hearted man, therefore felt a good deal uncomfortable in prospect of the grief likely to be manifested by the four or five hundred negroes belonging to the plantation, and particularly the house-servants, when called upon to part with little Elsie.

Both Mrs. Murray and Mildred had spoken to him of their strong attachment to the child, and his own observation had told him the same thing. He knew that they almost idolized her, and would feel her removal as a heavy blow. Desirous to lighten the stroke, he determined to allow Elsie to make a farewell present to each, and engaged Mildred and Mrs. Murray to assist her in preparing a list of suitable articles to be sent for. The child, know ing nothing of her grandfather's reasons for permitting this unusual outlay, was highly delighted.

It was Mr. Dinsmore's will that his plans with regard to Elsie should be kept secret from her and the servants until near the end of his visit, still some weeks distant.

Those weeks flew fast to Mildred, spent in a round of innocent, restful enjoyments, marred only by the knowledge that they must be so fleeting.

The day set for the departure from Viamede was drawing near when the sight of some of the needful preparations revealed the truth to the house-servants, and from them the sad tidings quickly spread to the field-hands, causing great grief and consternation.

Elsie was perhaps the last to learn the truth. She was running through the lower hall one morning soon after breakfast, when Aunt Phillis suddenly caught her in her arms, and holding her tight, covered the little fair face with kisses and tears.

"Why, Aunt Phillis, what's the matter?" asked the child, winding her small arms, so plump and white, about the woman's neck; "what makes you cry? is you sick?"

"O, honey, darlin'," sobbed the disconsolate

creature, " it's heap wus dan dat! Dey's gwine
to carry you 'way, bressed darlin' pet · 'way
off Norf, where Aunt Phillis won't neber see
yo' sweet face no mo'. Oh, dear! oh, dear!"

"No, no!" cried the child, struggling to
release herself. "Elsie's not goin' 'way, Aunt
Phillis. Where's mammy? I want mammy!"

Aunt Chloe came at the call, and Elsie ran
into her arms, crying in a frightened way
"Mammy, mammy, is dey going to take me
'way? Mammy, don't let dem!"

"Darlin', your ole mammy neber leave
you!" Aunt Chloe said soothingly, evading the
question she could not answer as she wished.

"Elsie doesn't want to go 'way!" sobbed
the child. "Dis is Elsie's home, dis is Elsie's
house. Elsie wants to stay here wis Aunt
Phillis and all Elsie's people! O, mammy,
mammy, does Elsie have to go?"

"Don't cry, honey, don't, darlin' pet; you
won't have to go 'way from mammy; mammy
'll go 'long, too," was all Aunt Chloe could
say.

The house-servants were crowding around
them, all weeping and wailing, and the little
girl seemed quite inconsolable.

Mildred heard and came to the rescue.

"Darling child," she said, kneeling on the

carpet by Elsie's side, and softly stroking the beautiful hair, "you are going to your papa's home; and perhaps you will see him there before long; and I think you will come back to Viamede some day."

At that the little head was lifted, and a smile broke like a sunbeam through the rain of tears.

"Papa!" she exclaimed, "will Elsie see her dear papa dere?   Den I won't cry any more!" and she wiped away her tears. "Don't cry, Aunt Phillis and Aunt Sally, and de rest of you; my papa will bring me back again."

"Dat be a long time off!" muttered Aunt Phillis, shaking her head as she moved slowly away.

"Roselands, your grandpa's and papa's home, is a very pretty place," Mildred went on, still caressing the shining curls, "and there are little boys and girls there that Elsie can play with."

"Brothers and sisters for me?" asked the little one joyously.

"Your papa's brothers and sisters, nice playfellows for you," Mildred answered. "There is Enra, who is just a baby girl, only two years old."

"I's four, I's big girl," put in the child.

"Yes; and Walter is past three, nearly as

old as you; and what nice plays you can have together."

" Yes, I want to take him a present; and one for the baby, and—what's dere names? de other children ? "

Mildred went over the list, and the baby girl repeated her wish to take a gift to each.

" We will ask your grandpa about it," Mildred said.

"Has dey dot a mamma?" was the next query; and that being answered in the affirmative, the wish was expressed that she, too, should be remembered with a pretty present, and that Cousin Milly would ask grandpa's permission for all these purchases.

Mildred took an early opportunity to do so.

" Who has put that nonsense into the child's head ? " he asked in some vexation.

"No one, uncle; it was entirely her own idea; perhaps suggested by the thought of her proposed gifts to those she leaves behind."

"Very likely; but let her forget it. I do not want to encourage her spending money upon my family."

" But her heart is very full of it, uncle, and I really think it would help to reconcile her to leaving Viamede. I'm afraid, uncle, that is going to be a hard trial for the little creature; for she dearly loves her home, and her people, as she calls the negroes."

"She will soon forget it all, and perhaps like Roselands quite as well. Childish griefs are not lasting."

"But terribly hard while they do last, uncle. I am not so old yet as to have forgotton that."

"No?" he said with a smile, followed by a sigh. "Ah, well, I'm sorry for the little thing, but don't see how it can be helped."

"But you will lessen the trial by humoring her in this and everything else that is reasonable?" persisted Mildred, in her most persuasive tone.

"Well, well, if I must, I must, I suppose! What an excellent advocate you are. But really I feel ashamed to allow it."

"Ah, uncle, it's your turn now," said Mildred, laughing. "I had mine in Philadelphia. But isn't Elsie rich enough to be allowed to spend such an amount on her own gratification?"

"Humph! what amount, pray? Ah, I have you there?" he added, laughing at her perplexed look.

"Not so fast, uncle!" she returned, brightening. "I can be definite. May she spend two hundred dollars for this?"

" No."

" One hundred and fifty, then ? "

" H'm! I don't know : we'll see about it when we get to New Orleans."

" Then I may tell her that she is to be allowed to buy presents for them ? "

" Yes. Now, don't make me commit myself any further."

After this Mildred talked a great deal to the little girl about the children at Roselands, the games and romps she would have with them, what should be bought for them, and how pleased they would be with her gifts. Also of all she was likely to see on her journey that would be new and interesting : how nice it was that Mrs. Murray and mammy were to go with her ; grandpa, too, and Cousin Milly ; and that the dear Saviour and " her own sweet, pretty mamma," would be just as near her there in her new home as at Viamede.

It was thus she tried to tide the darling over the trial that awaited her in the sundering of the tender ties that bound her to the home of her early infancy.

Those were April days with the baby girl, from the time of Aunt Phillis's unfortunate revelation of what awaited her until the blow fell.

They were to leave in the morning, though not at a very early hour, and at Elsie's request the field-hands were excused from work for the half day, and directed to come up to the house soon after the family breakfast, to say good-bye to their little mistress.

They gathered in a crowd in the rear of the mansion. The family party—Mr. Dinsmore, Mildred, Elsie and Mrs. Murray—were assembled upon the back veranda, where stood a table piled with the goods to be distributed. The little girl sat beside it on her mammy's lap, Mildred and Mrs. Murray near at hand to give their assistance; the overseer, standing on the topmost step, called the roll, and each, coming forward in answer to his name, received a gift presented by the child herself, and was allowed to kiss the small white hand that bestowed it.

This was esteemed a great privilege, and many held the hand a moment, dropping tears as well as kisses upon it, and heaping blessings on the head of the little fair one; pouring out their lamentations, also, over her approaching departure, till at length her tears fell so fast that her grandfather interfered, forbidding any further allusion to that subject, on pain of having to receive their gifts from some other hand,

No one was neglected, no one had been forgotten, but each, from octogenarian, no longer able or expected to work, down to the babe of a few days, received a gift of substantial worth to him or her; after which came a liberal distribution of pies, cakes, candies and fruits.

The baby girl dried her tears, and even laughed right merrily more than once, as she watched them at their feast. But her grief burst forth afresh, and with redoubled violence, when the time came for the final parting, and the house-servants gathered, weeping, about her.

She embraced them in turn, again and again, clinging about their necks, crying, " Oh, Elsie can't go 'way and leave you! Elsie must stay wis you! Elsie loves you! Elsie loves her own dear home, and can't go 'way !" while they strained the little form to their hearts with bitter wailing and lamentation.

To Mildred the scene was heart-rending, and her tears fell fast; Mrs. Murray was scarcely less moved; Aunt Chloe was sobbing, and tell-tale moisture stood in Mr. Dinsmore's eyes.

"Come, come," he said at length, speaking somewhat gruffly, to hide his emotion, " we have had enough of this! there's no use in fretting over what cannot be helped. Elsie's father will be bringing her back one of these days; so dry your eyes, Aunt Phillis, and all of you. The boat is waiting, the captain wanting to be off. Are you quite ready, ladies?"

Receiving an answer in the affirmative, "Then let us go on board at once," he said, and would have taken his little granddaughter in his arms; but Aunt Phillis begged the privilege of carrying her to the pier. Then with one last, long, clinging embrace, she resigned her to her nurse.

"Dere, honey darlin', dry yo' eyes and don' cry no mo'. Wipe de tears away so you can see your home while we's goin' 'long past de orchard and fields," Aunt Chloe said, standing on the deck and lifting the child high in her arms. "An' look, pet, dere's all de darkies standing 'long de sho' to see de boat move off; and dat's de way dey'll stand and watch it, when you and ole mammy comes back."

Yes, there they were, gathered in a crowd close to the water's edge, weeping and wailing, Aunt Phillis in the foreground wringing her hands, and with the big tears rolling fast down her cheeks.

The child saw and stretched out her arms to her with a cry of mingled love and distress;

tnen, as the boat swept onward, turned and buried her face in her mammy's bosom.

Mildred saw it all through eyes dimmed with tears. "Don't cry, darling!" she whispered to Elsie. "Think about the time when your dear papa will bring you back. Now lift up your head and look again at your beautiful home."

"Will my own papa bring Elsie back and live here wis me?" asked the little one, lifting her head as she was bidden, and smiling through her tears, as she gazed out over the lovely landscape.

"I hope so," Mildred said. "And you mustn't forget what a nice time we're going to have in New Orleans, buying the pretty things for the children at Roselands."

That was a wise suggestion, very helpful in cheering the sorrowful baby heart. In the discussion of the momentous and interesting questions what those gifts should be, and in what sort of places they would be found, she presently grew quite cheerful and animated.

A wonderful new world opened upon the baby eyes as they neared the city. She was filled with eager curiosity and delight, manifested in ways so entertaining and winsome, and by questions showing so much native wit, that her grandfather's heart warmed toward her Then, wherever they went he found her attracting so much attention, by reason of her beauty, sweetness and intelligence, that he grew proud of her in spite of himself.

Chapter Twenty-fifth.

"Envy is but the smoke of low estate,
Ascending still against the fortunate."
—LORD BROOKE.

"MAMMA, what's the matter?" asked Adelaide Dinsmore.

They were at the breakfast table; Mrs. Dinsmore was reading a letter from her husband, and Adelaide had been studying her face the while, noting the gathering frown upon the brow, the flushing of the cheek, the compression of the lips that spoke of increasing anger.

"Matter? I was never so provoked in my life!" cried Mrs. Dinsmore, crushing the letter passionately in her hands, then tearing it into bits. "The idea of bringing that child here! and not merely for a visit (which would be bad enough), but to stay permanently. I don't know what your father can be thinking of! It seems it's not enough that I've been tormented with a stepson, but I must have a step—"

"Step what, mamma?" from all three of the little girls, as she broke off abruptly, leaving her sentence unfinished.

"Nonsense! be quiet, will you!" she answered angrily.

They waited a moment for her passion to cool; then Adelaide began again.

"What child, mamma? Is papa coming home, and going to bring a child with him?"

"Yes; your brother Horace's child! You may as well know it first as last, I suppose."

Three pairs of eyes opened wide with amazement, three young voices crying out together, "Brother Horace's child! why, mamma, what can you mean? We didn't know he had any. We never even heard that he was married!"

"Of course you didn't," said Mrs. Dinsmore, pushing away her plate; "and probably you never would if this child hadn't been stubbornly determined to live in spite of losing her mother before she was a week old.

"No; we were never proud of the match, and had kept the thing quiet; but now it will be a nine days' wonder to the neighborhood, and the whole story will have to come out."

" Then you might as well tell it to us," was Adelaide's sage rejoinder. " Come, mamma, do, I'm dying of curiosity."

" It can be told in a few words," said Mrs Dinsmore, in a tone of wearied impatience. " Five years ago Horace went on a visit to New Orleans, met an orphan girl of large fortune, fell in love with her, and persuaded her to marry him. The thing was clandestine, of course ; for they were mere boy and girl. They lived together for two or three months, then her guardian, who had been away, came home, found it out, and was furious.

" He carried the girl off, nobody knew where ; your father sent Horace North to college, and some months afterward we heard that the girl was dead and had left a baby. She's four years old now ; the guardian is dead, and your father is bringing her home to live.

" There, I've given you the whole story, and don't intend to be bothered with any more questions."

" But, mamma," burst out the children, who had listened with breathless interest, " you haven't told us her name, or when they are coming?"

" Her name is Elsie, and they will be here in about a week. There, now, not another ques-

312   MILDRED AT ROSELANDS.

tion. I'm bored to death with the subject."

"Four years old; why, she's just a baby,' remarked Adelaide to her sisters. "Let's go tell mammy the news, and that she's going to have another baby to take care of."

"No, she's not," said Mrs Dinsmore sharply; "the child has a mammy of her own that's coming with her."

"What relation is she to us, Ade?" asked Lora.

"Who? the black woman? None to me, I'm sure," laughed Adelaide.

"You know I didn't mean that!" Lora retorted, in a vexed tone.

"Why, we're aunts!" exclaimed Louise. "Now, isn't that funny? And mamma's a grandmother! that's funnier still!" she added, with a burst of laughter.

Mrs. Dinsmore was in the act of leaving the room, but turned back to say wrathfully, "No such thing! the child is not related to me in the least. So don't let me hear any more of that nonsense."

"Mamma's mad," laughed Louise, "mad enough to shake me, I do believe. She loesn't like to be thought old enough to be a grandmother"

"May be she isn't," said Lora. Horace was a pretty big boy when papa and mamma were married; wasn't he, Ade?"

"I can't remember before I was born," Adelaide answered teasingly.

"Well, if you don't know about anything but what has happened since you were born, you don't know much," Lora retorted with spirit. "But I'll go and ask mammy. She'll know, for she was here before he was born."

It was a lovely spring day, and from the windows of the breakfast-room they could see Aunt Maria, the old colored woman who had been nurse in the family ever since the birth of Mr. Dinsmore's eldest child, and whom they all called mammy, walking about under the trees in the garden, with Baby Enna in her arms, while Arthur and Walter gambolled together on the grass near by.

" Ki, chillens! what's de mattah?" she exclaimed, pausing in her walk, as the three little girls came bounding toward her in almost breathless excitement.

"O, mammy!" they cried, all speaking at once, "did you know that brother Horace was married and has a baby girl? and that papa's bringing her home to live?"

"Ki chillens, what you talkin' 'bout?" returned the old woman, incredulously. "You's tryin' to fool your ole mammy."

"No, no, indeed, mammy! it's all so: mamma has just been telling us;" and they went on to repeat substantially what they had just learned from their mother.

Aunt Maria was an intensely interested and astonished listener; and they had several others before their story was finished; Arthur and Walter came running up to ask what it was all about, and two or three servants also joined the little group.

"You look pleased, mammy; are you, really?" asked Adelaide.

"To be sure I is, chile," returned the old nurse, with a broad grin of satisfaction. "Marse Horace one ob my chillens, and I'll be mighty glad to see his little chile."

The news spread rapidly among the servants, and formed their principal topic of conversation from that time till the arrival of their master and his young charge.

On leaving the breakfast-room Mrs. Dinsmore bent her steps toward the nursery. She found it untenanted except by a housemaid, who was engaged in putting it in order for the day.

"Go and tell Mrs. Brown that I wish to

speak to her immediately," commanded the mistress, dropping into an easy chair.

" Yes, missus," and the girl disappeared, to return shortly, accompanied by the house-keeper.

"You have heard from Mr. Dinsmore?" remarked the lady inquiringly, addressing Mrs. Brown.

" Yes, ma'am. He writes that Mrs. Murray, the housekeeper at Viamede, has consented to take my place for the coming year."

"Yes; I'm afraid she won't suit me as well. It's a great pity you should have got such a notion in your head; I mean as to the neces-sity or desirability of going away. I don't think you'll find a healthier place anywhere else than Roselands."

"I've no fault to find with the place ma'am; but I need rest, the doctor says, from the care and—"

"Dr. Barton's full of notions!" inter-rupted Mrs. Dinsmore impatiently. "Well, you'll stay, I suppose, until this Mrs. Mur-ray learns from you about the ways of the house?"

"Yes, ma'am; since you wish it."

Mrs. Dinsmore gave her orders for the day, as usual, then said, " There's another thing,

Mrs. Brown. You have probably heard that Mr. Dinsmore is bringing a child with him?"

"Yes, ma'am; he mentioned it in his letter to me, saying that a room must be got ready for her and her nurse."

"That is what I was coming to."

Mrs. Dinsmore arose and opened a door leading into an adjoining apartment.

"This room will answer very well. Have the trunks and boxes carried to the attic, the floor, paint, and window washed, a single bedstead, washstand, bureau, and two or three chairs brought in, and put up a white muslin curtain to the window."

But, ma'am—Mrs. Dinsmore—" and Mrs. Brown looked almost aghast at her employer.

"Well?" exclaimed the latter, with sharpness.

"Excuse me, ma'am, but isn't—I understood that the little lady was Mr. Dinsmore's granddaughter, and—and quite an heiress."

"Well, and supposing she is all that?"

"I beg pardon, Mrs. Dinsmore, but isn't the room rather small? Only one window, too, and I presume she's been used to—"

"It makes no difference what she's been used to, and you are presuming too far. You will be good enough to see that my orders are car-

ried out at once;" and Mrs. Dinsmore was
sweeping from the room in her most dignified
style, but turned at the door to add, " A cot bed
can be put up here for the nurse, and the door
left open between at night:" then sailed ma-
jestically down the hall.

" Dear, dear, whatever will Mr. Dinsmore
say to having his granddaughter put into such
a hole as that!" exclaimed the housekeeper,
half to herself, and half to the housemaid.
" Well, it can't be helped. I'll just have to do
the best I can, and tell him 'twasn't my fault.
Sally, do you go down and send up two of
the boys to carry away these trunks; and tell
Aunt Phœbe to heat a kettle of soft water for
the scrubbing."

Mrs. Brown did her best; had the room
thoroughly cleaned, neatly papered and carpeted, a set of pretty cottage furniture carried
in, put a lace curtain to the window, looped it
back with pink ribbon, made up the bed in the
daintiest fashion, and on the day the travelers
were expected to arrive, decorated the small
apartment profusely, with the loveliest and most
fragrant flowers that could be found, trans-
forming it into a bower of beauty.

Mrs. Dinsmore paid no attention to her
proceedings, but the children watched them

with interest, wondering the while that so mean a room had been selected for their little niece.

They were quite amused and gratified with the idea of being aunts and uncles, and if left to themselves would have been disposed to welcome the little stranger warmly ; but the slighting, sneering way in which their mother alluded to her and her mother's family, presently impressed them with the idea that she was to be looked upon as an object of contempt, if not as a positive disgrace to the family.

They reasoned among themselves, the older ones at least, that probably Horace thought so too, or he would have told them about her.

But when they saw the carriage which was bringing her, their father, and Mildred from the city, actually rolling up the avenue, all this was forgotten, and they rushed to the door to meet them, filled with curiosity and delight.

There was a tumultuous embracing of their father and cousin ; then they turned to look at the child.

What they saw was a small, fairy-like figure in the arms of a pleasant-looking, middle-aged colored woman, a delicate oval face, tinted with the loveliest shades of pink and white, framed in by a mass of golden ringlets, and lighted by a pair of eyes of the softest hazel, which were gazing half shyly, half eagerly at them.

"Oh, you darling, you pretty darling!" cried Adelaide, reaching her with a bound, and giving her a vigorous hug and kiss. "Do you know that I'm your auntie? and don't you think it's funny?"

The embrace was instantly returned, a beautiful smile breaking over the sweet little face, while the baby voice cooed, "Yes, Elsie loves you."

"Don't teaze the child, Adelaide. Children, let her alone," said Mrs. Dinsmore, sharply.

But no one seemed to hear or heed; children and servants had gathered round in quite a little crowd, and were hugging and kissing and making much of her, examining her with as much curiosity as if she were a new specimen of the genus homo, calling her "Brother Horace's little girl," "Massa Horace's baby," remarking upon the beauty of her complexion, her eyes, her hair, the pretty round white shoulders and arms, and the tiny, shapely hands and feet.

"They'll hae the bairn fairly puffed up wi' vanity Miss Mildred!" exclaimed Mrs. Murray in a dismayed aside to our heroine.

"Never mind," whispered Mildred, joyously; "I'm only too glad she should have such a welcome, the darling! and I don't believe it will hurt her in the least."

"There, children, and the rest of you, tha' will do," said Mr. Dinsmore with authority "The child is tired with her long journey Carry her to her room, Aunt Chloe, and let her have something to eat and a nap."

Aunt Chloe obeyed; Mildred hurried after to see the child comfortably established, and then dress herself for dinner; Mrs. Brown invited Mrs. Murray to her new quarters, and Mr. Dinsmore, waiting only to give an order to his body servant, hastened after the little girl and her attendant, following the sound of their voices; for the child was prattling to her mammy and Mildred, and they were answering her innocent questions and remarks.

"Dis my little missus's room?" Mr. Dinsmore heard Aunt Chloe exclaim in a tone of astonishment and contempt, as the little party, guided by Sally, the housemaid, reached the door of the room selected by Mrs. Dinsmore.

He hurried forward. "What, this pigeonhole?" he exclaimed, turning wrathfully to the girl. "Who bade you bring the young lady, Mr. Horace's daughter, here?"

"Missus tole de housekeeper fix dis room

fo' de little lady, massa, ' replied the girl, trembling with affright.

"Stupid, you must have misunderstood her," he said. " This way, Aunt Chloe."

The room to which he conducted them adjoined that appropriated to Mildred, and was equally large, airy, and cheerful; equally well furnished.

Aunt Chloe surveyed it with a look of relief and satisfaction, and bidding her send Sally for whatever was wanted for the child, Mr. Dinsmore left them and went down to his wife.

She read displeasure in his countenance, and drew out her handkerchief in preparation for her usual mode of defense.

" Pray, madam," he demanded in irate tone, " by whose orders was that cubby-hole prepared for the use of Horace's child ? "

" That very nice little room next the nursery was the one selected by myself," she answered with dignity.

" Nice little room, indeed ! " he returned with scorn ; " ten feet by twelve ! that for one born in a palace and reared, thus far, in the very lap of luxury ! "

" Plenty good enough and big enough for old Grayson's grandchild ! " observed the wife, turning up her aristocratic nose in supreme contempt.

"Madam, she is also my grandchild, and heiress in her own right to over a million."

Mrs. Dinsmore's look expressed, first, astonishment, then jealous rage and envy. "And the very incarnation of beauty!" she muttered between her clenched teeth. "What did you bring her here for—to cast our children into the shade? I hate her! What have you been doing? where have you put her?"

"In the blue room."

"The blue room! one of the very best in the house! the blue satin damask cushions of the chairs and sofas are so handsome and delicate! and to think of the sun being let in to fade them, and a baby rubbing its shoes over them, and scattering greasy crumbs on them; and that exquisite carpet! It's too trying for flesh and blood to stand!" and the handkerchief went up to her eyes.

"It's not worth while to distress yourself," he remarked coolly; "her income is quite sufficient to allow of it's being refurnished at double the cost every six months if necessary."

"You ought to be ashamed of yourself, Mr. Dinsmore, throwing up her wealth to me in that style!" sobbed the much-tried and very ill-used woman.

Little Elsie was brought down to the draw-

ing-room after tea, Mildred leading her in,
while Aunt Chloe followed, bearing a paste-
board box.

Fresh pangs of envy and jealousy assailed
Mrs. Dinsmore at sight of the little fair one,
now rested and refreshed, beautifully and taste-
fully attired, and looking even more bewitch-
ingly lovely than on her arrival.

Running to her grandfather, she asked coax-
ingly, " Please, grandpa, may Elsie dive de fings
now ? "

" As well now as any time," he said, not
unkindly, and she ran back to Mildred, who had
taken the box from Aunt Chloe, and now opened
and held it so that the child could handle the
contents.

" This is the one for Enna's mamma," Mildred whispered, pointing to a jewel case ; " I
would give it first."

The small white hands seized it, the soft
brown eyes glanced about the room till they
rested upon the figure of a richly-dressed lady
in an easy chair ; then the little twinkling feet
tripped across, and with a shy look, up in the
not too pleasant face, the case was laid in her
lap, the baby voice lisping sweetly, " Please,
Enna's mamma, Elsie wants to dive you dis."

Mrs. Dinsmore started with surprise,

opened the case hastily, and seeing a very handsome gold bracelet lying there, condescended to
smile and murmur a few words of thanks.

But the little one had not waited for them ;
back to Mildred she ran in eager haste to finish
the work of presenting her love tokens to these
new-found relatives ; a handsome gold ring to
each of the three little girls (received with kisses,
thanks and exclamations of delight), and toys
for the others, which seemed to give equal satisfaction.

Chapter Twenty-sixth.

"Sweet beauty sleeps upon thy brow,
And floats before my eyes ;
As meek and pure as doves art thou,
Or beings of the skies."

—ROBERT MORRIS.

"Do you like it, aunt ? " asked Mildred, approaching Mrs. Dinsmore, as she was in the act of clasping the bracelet on her arm.

"Yes, it's very handsome ; but I think there might as well have been a pair of them."

"Ah ! " returned Mildred with a smile, directed toward Mr. Dinsmore ; "little Elsie would have been glad to make it so, but uncle held the purse-strings, and was inexorably determined that it should be but one."

"Just like him ! " said the wife, snappishly.

"My dear, I felt extremely mean in allowing so much as I did to be spent upon my family," he said with a gravity that was almost stern.

"I don't see why you need," she replied,

with irritation, " sacrificing the comfort of your family, as you are, by taking her in."

" I must confess," he returned, " that I see no sacrifice about it. The child will not be the slightest expense to us. But rather the reverse; nor will her presence in the house add in the very least to your cares."

" The children seem well pleased with their gifts," Mildred remarked, giving him a cheery smile, as she moved away toward them, gathered in a little throng about Elsie, amusing themselves by making her talk; asking her questions, and bidding her pronounce their names in turn, with the prefix of aunt or uncle.

" You're the darlingest little thing that ever was ! " Adelaide exclaimed, catching her in her arms, and kissing her again and again.

" She's too pretty ; nobody will ever look at us when she's by.   I heard mamma say so," muttered Louise, discontentedly.

" Pooh ! " what's the use of talking in that way ! " said Lora. " We can hide her up-stairs when we want to be looked at."

" Of course,' said Mildred, laughing; " and being such a mere baby, I don't think you need fear that she will prove a serious rival."

" I'm her uncle," remarked Arthur, drawing himself up, with dignity; "say Uncle Arthur again, baby girl."

"I isn't a baby," she said, smiling up into his face. "Elsie's a big girl now; Enna's de baby. Pretty baby! Elsie loves you!" she added, lovingly stroking Enna's hair.

"It's high time those children were in bed,' said Mrs. Dinsmore, from the other side of the room. "Aunt Maria, take Enna and the boys to the nursery."

Aunt Chloe, not slow to take a hint, picked up her nursling and followed the other woman, Elsie looking back, and kissing her hand to her grandfather, with a pleasant "Good-night, grandpa; good-night, Enna's mamma, and all de folks."

Mildred went with them to enjoy a little talk and play with the child, as had been her custom at Viamede, but did not venture to stay long, lest Mrs. Dinsmore should be displeased at her absenting herself from the drawing-room on this first evening after her return.

On going down again, she found Mr. Landreth there. He spent the evening, and made himself very agreeable. Mildred was quite full of Viamede, and its little heiress, and he seemed much interested in all she had to say about them.

Mr. Landreth was a favorite with Mrs. Dinsmore; she considered him an excellent match in point of wealth and family, possessed also of the added recommendations of good education, polished address and genial disposition.

He had been a frequent visitor to Roselands in the past months, and she had spared no pains to show off to him the attractions of her nieces, and throw him as much as possible into their society; at the same time adroitly keeping Mildred in the background.

But the young man was sufficiently keen-sighted to see through her schemes, and while seemingly falling in with them, in reality reserved all his admiration for Mildred; who on her part was taken up with other interests, and thought of him only as a pleasant acquaintance, whose visits to the house meant nothing to her.

Mrs. Dinsmore had been disappointed by her failure to secure him for one or the other of her nieces; but they were now engaged, and having come to have as warm a liking for our heroine as it was in her selfish nature to entertain for any one not connected with herself by ties of blood, she desired, as the next best thing, to bring about a match between her and Mr. Landreth.

But Mildred did not second her efforts,

showing no particular preference for Mr. Landreth's society above that of any one of the half dozen or more other unmarried gentlemen who frequented the house.

She treated them all courteously, but gave encouragement to none, seeming far more interested in little Elsie, and in the studies almost discontinued during her stay at Viamede, but taken up again with renewed zeal directly on her return to Roselands.

But Mr. Landreth was not to be discouraged; he paid court to Elsie, learning soon to love the little creature for her own sweet sake, and managed after a time to associate himself with several of Mildred's pursuits.

The time had now arrived when, according to the original plan, Mildred was to return home, and those who loved her there were looking forward with eager impatience for her coming.

But Mr. Dinsmore wrote to her parents, entreating that he might be allowed to keep her some months longer, and bringing forward several cogent reasons why his request should be granted; Mildred was improving in health, making the best use of opportunities to perfect herself in accomplishments, etc.; was a most pleasant companion to himself and wife, ought not to be permitted to undertake the long journey alone ; and at present no suitable escort could be found.

The parents carefully weighed his arguments, and for their child's sake finally gave consent, albeit somewhat reluctantly.

Mildred was both glad and sorry, having a yearning desire for home and its dear occupants, but at the same time feeling that the parting from wee Elsie would be very sad ; so tender was the attachment that had sprung up between herself and the motherless babe.

Pity was a large element in Mildred's love for the child, and that increased as the weeks and months rolled on ; for both the grandfather and the young uncles and aunts, yielding gradually to Mrs. Dinsmore's baleful influence, treated her with less kindness and consideration ; while Mrs. Dinsmore's tyranny was such that not unfrequently Mildred could scarce refrain from expressing violent indignation.

The child was not subjected to blows, but angry looks and harsh words and tones, that to her sensitive spirit were worse than blows would have been to a more obtuse nature, were plentifully dealt out to her ; also ridicule, sneers and snubs.

And there was no respect shown to her rights of property · the other children might rob her of her toys, books and pictures, with entire impunity, if she ventured to carry them outside her own room ; Mrs. Dinsmore averring that if she showed them, and so excited a desire for them in the breasts of her children, she deserved to lose them.

" She is quite able to afford to present them with anything they want," she would add, " and I am not going to have them tormented with the sight of pretty things that are to be refused them."

Elsie was so unselfish and generous that, as a usual thing, she could be easily induced to give even what she highly valued ; but to have her possessions laid violent hands upon and forced from her outraged her sense of justice, and though she seldom offered much resistance, it often cost her many bitter tears.

She was a careful little body, who never destroyed anything, and her loving nature made her cling even to material things, in some instances, which she had owned and amused herself with for years; an old dollie, that she had loved and nursed from what was to her time immemorial, was so dear and precious, that no new one, however beautiful and fine, could possibly replace it. And a living pet took such a place in her heart from the first—a tame squirrel

that she had brought with her, and a white
dove given her by Mr. Landreth soon after her
arrival.

But all these were taken from her; the doll
had to be resigned to Enna, the dove to Walter,
and the squirrel to Arthur.

There was a short struggle each time, then
she gave it up and sobbed out her sorrow in her
mammy's arms, or on Mildred's sympathizing
bosom.

"Oh, Elsie wants to go back to her own
dear home!" she would cry. "Can't Elsie go
back? Must Elsie stay here, where dey take her
fings all away?"

Mildred at first hoped her uncle would interfere; but no, he did not enjoy contention
with his wife, and, like many another man,
could not understand how things of value so
trifling in his sight, could be worth so much to
the child.

He was willing to replace them, and thought
it only ill-temper and stubbornness when she
refused to be comforted in that manner.

It was a sore trial to the three hearts in
the house that loved her so dearly; but all they
could do was to soothe her with caresses and
assurances of their love, and of the love of Jesus,
and that if she bore her trials with meekness

and patience, returning good for evil to those who used her so ill, it would be pleasing to Him.

Mildred would talk to her of her papa, too, and the happy times she would have when he came home;—how he would love and pet and fondle her.

" For surely," she reasoned with herself, " he cannot possibly do otherwise when he sees how sweet and lovely she is."

The prospect seemed to give the little one intense pleasure, and she would often ask to be told " 'bout de time when Elsie's dear papa will come."

She would watch her grandfather, too, as he petted and fondled his little ones, with a wistful longing in the sweet brown eyes that brought tears to those of Mildred, and made her heart ache.

Chapter Twenty-sebenth.

"Wooing thee, I found thee of more value
Than stamps in gold, or sums in sealed bags;
And 'tis the very riches of thyself
That now I aim at."

—SHAKSPEARE.

EARLY in June, the Dinsmores repaired to the sea-shore, taking Mildred with them; also little Elsie and her mammy.

The whole summer was spent at watering-places, and Mr. Landreth was generally one of their party.

Mildred enjoyed it, the time spent at the sea-shore, especially, very much in a quiet way, taking no part in the gaieties of the fashionables, but delighting in walks and drives along the beach, and in boating and bathing.

Elsie was fond of a morning stroll on the beach, with "Cousin Milly," Aunt Chloe being always at hand to carry her pet when the little feet grew tired, and Mildred was never averse to the companionship of the sweet child. never in too great haste to accommodate her pace to that of the little one, or to stop to examine and explain whatever excited her curiosity, or to let her pick up sea-weed, shells and pebbles.

Sometimes the other children joined them; occasionally Mr. Landreth also. Later in the day he was almost sure to be Mildred's companion, unless she contrived to elude him.

This she attempted quite frequently toward the latter part of the summer, declining his attentions whenever she could, without positive rudeness.

At first he would not believe it was by design, but at length he could no longer shut his eyes to the fact, and, much disturbed and mortified, he determined to seek an explanation; he must know what was her motive—whether aversion to his society, or fear that he was trifling with her; and if the latter, it should speedily be removed; he would tell her what was the sober truth, that he esteemed and admired her above all the rest of her sex, and would be supremely happy if she would consent to be his wife.

They and their party had left the sea-shore for a fashionable resort among the mountains, where they had now been for a fortnight or more, and where they had found the elder Mr.

Landreth and his wife established for the season.

Mildred set out for a walk, one morning, directly after breakfast, taking Elsie and her nurse with her.

They found a cool, shady spot, beside a little brook, at the foot of a hill where the grass was green, and a rustic seat under a spreading tree invited to rest.

They sat down, and Elsie amused herself with throwing pebbles and bits of bark into the water.

"Aunt Chloe," Mildred said, presently, " I want to climb this hill, for the sake of the view ; so will leave you and Elsie here. I don't intend to be gone long, but if she gets tired waiting, you can take her back to the house, and I will follow."

So saying, she tripped away back to the road, made her ascent, seated herself upon a log, at a spot which commanded a fine view of the mountain, hill and vale, and taking out her drawing materials, was about to sketch the scene, when a voice addressed her.

"Good-morning, Miss Keith. I am happy to have come upon you just now, and alone.

"I'm quite out of breath with climbing the hill," the voice went on, as Mildred, turning her head, recognized Mrs. Landreth, responded to her greeting, and made room for her on the log. "Thank you; yes, I will sit down here beside you, for I want to rest and to have a little talk with you."

"I am at your service, Mrs. Landreth," Mildred said, closing her sketch-book, recalling as she did so her companion's formerly expressed opinion that such employment was a sinful waste of time, and anticipating a lecture on that subject.

However, the good woman's thoughts were, at that moment, too full of a more important theme to allow her to so much as notice with what the young girl had busied herself.

"My dear," she began, "I have a strong liking and high respect for you; because you seem to me sincerely desirous to do right and live in a Christian way, according to your light. You are gayer, of course, in your dress than I can think quite consistent; but we don't all see alike; and I should be rejoiced to receive you into the family if that might be without the danger to you—spiritually—which it involves."

Mildred rose, her cheeks burning, her eyes flashing.

"When I have shown my desire to enter

your family, Mrs. Landreth, it will be time
enough to—"

"Ah, my dear, my dear, you quite misun-
derstand me," interrupted the older lady.
'Except for your own sake and your duty as a
Christian to marry only in the Lord, I should
be delighted. And I've never felt at all sure
that Charlie could get you; but I see plainly
that he wants you; and so it seemed my duty
to warn you not to take him."

Mildred was very angry. Drawing herself
up to her full height, and speaking with
hauteur, "Excuse me, madam," she said, "if
I venture to remind you that unasked advice is
seldom acceptable; and if I add that it is especially unpalatable when it involves the meddling with matters too delicate for even the
most intimate friend to allude to uninvited."

"What a temper! I begin to think you
are none too good for him after all," grimly
commented Mrs. Landreth, rising in her turn.
"Good-morning, miss," and she stalked away
down the hill, while Mildred dropped upon
the grass, and hiding her face in her hands,
indulged in a hearty cry.

It was a mixture of emotions that brought
he tears in those plentiful showers; anger
burned still in her breast, yet at the same time

she was bitterly remorseful on account of it, sorry and ashamed that she had so disgraced her Christian profession; bringing reproach upon the Master's cause; and—ah, what meant the pang that meddling woman's words had caused? could it be the fear that duty called her to resign that which had become very dear to her heart? Alas, yes! it cried out with a yearning, passionate cry for this love that she must reject, if, indeed, it was offered her.

Did he, indeed, love her? Oh, what joy! what bliss! But, oh, the bitter anguish if she must put that cup of joy aside untasted! How could she? yet how dare she do otherwise? The Bible did speak of marrying only in the Lord; it did say, "Be ye not unequally yoked together with unbelievers."

Some one knelt on the grass at her side, gently lifted up her head and took her hands in his

"Don't, darling; I cannot bear to see tears in those dear eyes. I know all—I met her, and she told me. How dared she so wound your delicacy! But it is true that I love you · yes, a thousand times better than she can imagine! and that I am utterly unworthy of you. But, Mildred, dearest, sweetest, best of women, give me a little hope, and I will try to become all you can ask."

She could not speak. She tried to hide her blushing face, and to withdraw her hands; but he held them fast, and continued to pour out earnest pleadings and passionate expres sions of love and devotion.

"I cannot, oh, I cannot!" she stammered at last. "I'm afraid she is right. Not, oh, not that I am any better than you! but—but we are traveling different roads, and 'how can two walk together except they be agreed?'"

"I would never interfere with your religion," he said. "I know it is different from that which makes my poor uncle's home the most desolate place on earth. O, Mildred, think that you may be the saving of me! I am willing to walk in your road if you will show me the way; even to join the church at once if that will satisfy you.'

She looked up wistfully into his face. "Ah, Charlie—Mr. Landreth—is that your idea of what it is to be a Christian? Ah, it is more, much more.

"'With the heart man believeth unto right eousness'—gets the righteousness of Christ put upon him, imputed to him, while holy living proves the reality of the change, the saving

nature of his faith—' and with the mouth con·
fession is made unto salvation.'

"Do you not see that conversion must come
before joining the church ?"

"I don't understand these things," he said;
"but I am willing to learn. O, Mildred, be my
wife, and you may lead me whither you will!"

She shook her head sorrowfully, tears steal·
ing down her cheeks.

"I am too weak, too ready to stray from the
path myself, too easily led by those I—"

"Love?" he whispered eagerly, and bending
over her, as she paused in confusion, "O, Mildred, darling, say the sweet word! You do
love me! you do! I see it in your dear eyes,
and I will never despair. But speak the word,
dearest, once, just once!"

"Oh, Charlie!" she groaned, covering her
face, "I should learn to love you too well to
bear the thought that we were not to spend
eternity together."